W9-ANE-108

Fat Glenda Turns Fourteen

Fat Glenda TURNS FOURTEEN

by Lila Perl

CLARION BOOKS · NEW YORK

Clarion Books
a Houghton Mifflin Company imprint
215 Park Avenue South, New York, NY 10003

Printed in U.S.A.

Library of Congress Cataloging-in-Publication Data

Perl, Lila.
Fat Glenda turns fourteen / by Lila Perl.
p. cm.
Summary: Fourteen-year-old Glenda, extremely unhappy after regaining the pounds she worked so hard to lose, meets the very overweight Giselle and discovers the world of plus-size modeling, but she will have to stay fat to keep working as such a model.
ISBN 0-395-53341-4
[1. Weight control — Fiction. 2. Models, Fashion — Fiction.]
I. Title.
PZ7.P432Far 1991 90-40438
[Fic] — dc20

CIP
AC

BP 10 9 8 7 6 5 4 3 2 1

Fat Glenda Turns Fourteen

Chapter 1

Fourteen . . . and fat again. I stood in my room, gazing straight ahead into the full-length mirror and watched as my eyes filled up with tears. Slowly, two plump and glistening droplets began making their way down my newly pudgy cheeks. I stared at them in horror. Even my tears were fat!

Turning away in despair, I dropped with a thud into the dainty, flower-sprigged boudoir chair my mother had added to my room during the summer. "Just a comfy new welcome-home present for my little girl," my mother had declared when I'd returned from my summer job right after Labor Day.

"Little!" Sometimes my mother sounded like she'd been looking at me through the wrong end of a telescope. It was true, though, that I *had* been "littler" then — a whole eleven pounds thinner. But all *that* had been weeks and weeks ago. My gorgeous summer in the country was fading like a dream. It was hard to believe it had ever happened . . . except for the way I ached with loss and emptiness in a place just beneath my heart whenever I thought of it.

I dabbed at my eyes. A fat lot of good those memories did me now. Today was my fourteenth birthday, and in a little while my friends Patty and Mary Lou would be calling for me so we three could spend the day together.

"Dress kind of partylike, Glenda," Patty had advised me at school the day before, giving me a brisk nod. And Mary Lou, standing tall and skinny just behind Patty's short figure, had echoed, "Um-hmmm."

"Partylike?" I'd pounced. "What for? I told you I didn't want any kind of celebration. I thought we were going to hang out around town tomorrow, just like any other Saturday."

"Hanging out" around Havenhurst, the little suburban town on Long Island where I'd lived all my life, meant browsing in the shops over at the mall, dropping in at the video store, getting something to eat at a burger or pizza place — certainly nothing fancy.

Patty had looked almost annoyed with me. "It's still going to be a special day for you, Glenda. Don't you even *feel* birthday-ish?"

"No," I'd declared. "I can't be happy when I'm fat. That's why I said 'no party.' I'll celebrate when I lose all this weight I've been putting on. *If* I ever do."

Maybe it was just as well we'd agreed not to wear jeans today. Even my biggest, most stretched-out pair wouldn't zip all the way up anymore. I'd put on a new gray flannel skirt my mother had bought me and a blousy, oversize, pale pink sweater. And around my neck I'd fastened the antique gold locket on a chain that my mother and father had surprised me with as a birthday present that morning.

The musical chimes of the doorbell roused me from my mopiness. It was just past eleven o'clock and neither of my parents was at home. My father had gone off to his golf game, and my mother was busy with a fall fashion show and luncheon that she'd organized to raise money for one of her charity groups.

My mother's clubs were her "babies." She was always setting up bazaars and rummage sales, selling raffle tickets and planning bridge games and tea parties for worthy causes. It was amazing that anyone who charged around town the way she did, practically shooting off bolts of energy, could be as fleshy plump as she was. *Not* a very good omen for me — her one and only child.

The instant I opened the front door, Patty and Mary Lou burst excitedly into the living room. Like me, they were both wearing skirts, only theirs were almost minis. Mine couldn't afford to be.

"Ooh, Glenda, you look great. Not fat at all. I don't see what you're complaining about so much."

These words came from Mary Lou, who could fill up on a lettuce leaf and two gulps of air, and would definitely be a walking skeleton all her life.

Patty's dark eyes immediately fastened on my new locket. "Glenda, that's gorgeous. A birthday present?"

I nodded. "My mother found it in an antique jewelry shop." The locket *was* beautiful, a deep amber-gold with rich but delicate engraving all over its surface.

Patty fingered it carefully. "Does it open?"

"Of course," I said, touching the tiny clasp.

"What's in it?" Patty inquired almost slyly.

"Nothing," I answered.

Mary Lou arched her pale, swanlike neck to look over Patty's shoulder. "Nothin'?" she drawled. Mary Lou had lived in the South until she'd moved to Havenhurst a few years ago. She'd just finished spending the summer down there, working part-time in her aunt's dress shop. So her accent had gotten stronger again.

"You've *got* to put something inside of it, Glenda," Patty urged. "What about a picture of . . . Justin?"

I gave the locket a sharp tug, pulling it away from Patty's loosening grasp. Why had I ever even *told* my Havenhurst friends about Justin? How had I ever been stupid enough to believe that our relationship could last beyond Labor Day?

I'd met Justin last summer at the Thorn Ridge Inn, a New England country hotel where I'd been working as a waitress-in-training and Justin had been an assistant waiter. After a bumpy start, he and I had shared the most perfect summer — quiet walks by the mill stream, day-off bike rides to the nearest town for ice creams and sodas, moonlight swims, and long murmuring conversations. And in spite of all the luscious and tempting food at the inn, I'd managed to stay thin for Justin. His magical presence was all I'd needed to keep the ghost of formerly fat me far, far away.

In two heavenly words, Justin had been my "summer romance." Only now, halfway through October, it wasn't summer anymore!

Patty must have seen the sorrowful look in my eyes. "Listen, Glenda, it's not *that* long since he said he'd write to you. Everybody's been busy with getting back to school, buying winter clothes, making new friends —" Patty stopped herself abruptly. "Oops, I didn't mean that Justin already met somebody new. It's just that, well, boys are all terrible about writing. And what with his living as far away as Boston, you've got to admit it would be sort of expensive for him to start making phone calls. . . ."

Mary Lou tapped Patty gently on the shoulder. "We, um, ought to be going, Patty. You know, it's getting late."

"Late for what?" I asked, not that I minded getting off the subject of Justin. It was just too painful to think about him *and* about the way I'd been putting on something like an extra two pounds for every week that I hadn't heard from him. Because food, as always, was my consolation when things went wrong in my life.

My dearest friend, Sara Mayberry, had also spent the summer at the inn, where she and I had worked together and shared a room, as well as lots of confidences. Sara lived even farther away than Justin — in California — but *she'd* written. I suppose, though, that girl-and-girl friendships have always been a whole lot different from boy-and-girl friendships.

Mary Lou still hadn't answered my question about

what we were late for if we weren't doing anything special anyway. But I noticed that she and Patty were hastily zipping up their jackets. After a hazy, warmish September, the weather had turned clear and chilly.

I hated to think of the fat, lonely winter that probably lay ahead of me — and just when I'd turned fourteen, the truly grown-up age that I'd always dreamed of being.

Thirteen had always sounded almost as babyish to me as twelve. But fourteen sounded really sophisticated. It meant being a teen in every sense of the word — lively, independent, mature about boys, attractively dressed. . . . Only how was any of that going to be possible for somebody with the rapidly expanding body of a baby blimp?

"It might take a while before you hear from me, Glenda, because of all the mix-up about where I'll be going to school this fall. But I'll write you. You can count on it."

Those had been Justin's last words to me as we'd stood in the not-very-private lobby of the Thorn Ridge Inn, saying a final good-bye. Justin hadn't suggested that *I* write to him, but his broad grin had been totally reassuring. And, besides, he and I had a whole summer's history behind us.

Only how long was "a while"? Six weeks? Eight weeks? More?

As I prepared to leave the house with Patty and Mary Lou, a bizarre thought struck me. Suppose I never heard from Justin again. And suppose I kept right on gaining two pounds for every week of disappointment and disheartenment over the death of my summer romance. How long would it take before I became the fattest fourteen-year-old person on earth!

Chapter 2

"Where are we going, anyway?"

As soon as I'd locked the front door of my house behind us, Mary Lou and Patty had set off hurriedly down the street, with me following close behind.

Patty and Mary Lou exchanged glances and started to walk even faster.

"Don't bother answering, of course," I panted, already a little out of breath. Our "threesome" friendship had been like this ever since it had begun. Even though we often changed sides, it always seemed to be two against one. Today it definitely felt like them against me in some kind of conspiracy.

I could see Mary Lou nudge Patty with her shoulder. "Well, tell her. It's no secret . . . really."

"Guess not," Patty agreed, slowing down. She turned and fell into step beside me. The sidewalk was only wide enough for two people walking abreast — especially if I was one of them. "We thought we'd stop over at the video store first, Glenda. That okay with you?"

I nodded. "Makes no difference to me."

Ever since we'd each come back from our summer

jobs (Patty had been a mother's helper at a Long Island beach house), all I'd been hearing from Patty and Mary Lou had been arguments about when was the best time to meet boys over at the new video rental place that had opened in Havenhurst during the summer.

Patty insisted that Fridays after school were when most kids got together there to pick out their video movies for the weekend. But Mary Lou thought Saturdays were better. I suddenly began wondering if this was the real reason they'd both gotten dressed up in short skirts today.

Patty linked her arm chummily through mine. "We might, um, pick up a movie to watch on the VCR over at my house later, Glenda. If you want to, that is."

"Or," I tacked on knowingly, "you and Mary Lou might pick up a couple of cute new boys. . . .

Mary Lou overheard me and stopped short. In fact, I nearly fell headlong over her heels. She whirled around and shook a limp finger at me. "Say what you like, Glenda. It's very easy to get into conversations with boys when you're browsing among the shelves. You can talk about the different video movies. And nobody tells you *shush,* the way they do in the library.

"You know," she added almost accusingly, "Patty and I weren't as lucky as you. We didn't meet some wonderful summer boyfriend the way you did."

Justin again! Not that I needed reminding. Mary Lou wasn't mean but she could be thoughtless. So I just didn't answer her.

About five minutes later, we'd reached the business

section of Havenhurst and strolled as casually as we could into the new video store. At first glance, it looked like Mary Lou was going to lose her argument with Patty and be disappointed besides. All I could see in the store were some fathers with children in tow who were poking around in the kiddie section, probably looking for *Willy Wonka* or *Lady and the Tramp*. But then I'd only been in the store once before, so maybe I was wrong.

"Why don't you take Glenda on over to the horror section?" Patty suggested, pointing toward the rear wall. "There's something I promised to check on for my father at the rental desk. Be with you in a jiffy."

"That's a good idea," Mary Lou said, grabbing me by the arm while I was still looking over my shoulder at Patty. "Let's see if they got in *Blood Diner* yet. Some boys I was talkin' to here the other day told me about it. 'First they greet you, then they eat you!' That's how they advertise that video. Doesn't it sound just *too* disgustin', Glenda?"

I couldn't help squirming a little. "A diner where they chop the customers up for hamburger! That's almost enough to make *me* lose my appetite." I thought a moment. "But probably not quite."

It didn't take much to get Mary Lou turned off food, though. She wasn't just the world's pickiest eater; she was also the most squeamish person I knew.

"How come somebody like you is so interested in horror videos all of a sudden?" I asked her.

But Mary Lou didn't answer. She just kept dragging

me toward the shelves labeled Horror and Science Fiction. I think I already knew the answer, though. Mary Lou had come down with a delayed case of boy craziness over the summer. And those were the kinds of videos most boys would probably be looking for.

Sure enough, as we came around behind the last row of racks, we heard voices.

"Oh, my goodness," Mary Lou shrieked before I even had a chance to see who was there. "Look, Glenda. It's Roddy Fenton and . . . and . . ."

For several embarrassing seconds, nobody said anything. Then the stocky, dark-haired boy standing next to Roddy offered his name. "Ethan."

"Oh, hi," Mary Lou said breathlessly. "I do think I've seen you all around school, ah, Ethan. I'm Mary Lou Blenheim. And this here's my good friend, Glenda. Glenda Waite."

I nodded hello to the new boy. But I couldn't help blushing at the way Mary Lou had gone into her fancy-talking southern belle act to try to impress him.

We all knew Roddy Fenton, of course, from way back. He and I had once been bitter enemies, then pretty close friends, and lately . . . I just didn't know what. Once during the summer, while I'd been working at the Thorn Ridge Inn, Roddy had sent me a letter from the computer camp he was at. It was full of boring, technical details about the "exciting stuff" he was learning at camp, and I'd gotten the feeling he was turning into some kind of computer nerd, even though his looks had certainly improved in the last year or so.

He'd gone from a gawky, beaky-nosed little kid in oversize horn-rimmed eyeglasses to being tall, angular, and sort of interesting looking.

"Hey, Glenda," Roddy declared with a pleasantly surprised air. "You're looking great."

Great *big,* you mean, I thought to myself. I still didn't quite trust Roddy from back in the days when he'd teased me about being fat and called me Jelly Belly. Besides, I just couldn't help feeling self-conscious about all the weight I'd gained since the summer had ended. But maybe Roddy had forgotten how much thinner I'd been last June. He and I had hardly seen each other since school started because he was in a different ninth-grade homeroom from me.

"Today is Glenda's birthday," Mary Lou piped excitedly. "Honestly." She shifted her glance from Roddy to Ethan and let her eyes rest on Ethan's almost-too-perfect good looks. I noticed he was a little shorter than Mary Lou. But that didn't seem to bother her a bit.

"Yes, Glenda's sweet fourteen today," she went on, fluttering her blue-veined eyelids at Roddy's friend. When she wanted to look especially glamorous, Mary Lou dabbed Azure Stardust eye shadow on her lids to cover the veins and "bring out" her eyes. She was probably sorry now that she hadn't put any on today.

"Sweet fourteen?" Ethan remarked with a puzzled look. "I thought it was supposed to be sweet *sixteen.*"

Roddy gave Ethan a poke with his elbow. "You gotta get with it, man. Everything's speeded up nowadays." Roddy turned to me. "Congratulations, Glenda. You having a party?"

"No, I'm not," I replied quickly. "Patty and Mary Lou and I are just sort of spending the day together around town. But no party. Nothing."

Mary Lou giggled. "Oh, Glenda's so silly. She just doesn't want a . . . a fuss. But . . . but . . . if you-all would like to join us?" Mary Lou paused. "Um, later on, maybe . . ."

Roddy grinned. "Sure, why not? Maybe you girls would like to watch some creepy videos with us. We could have a real fright night. Scare city. Blow our minds."

I couldn't tell if Roddy was serious or not. Maybe he was just teasing again. At the same time, he started rattling off titles of horror videos. "Which ones should we check out? *Friday the Thirteenth, The Blob, Return of the Living Dead*?"

Ethan shook his head vigorously. "Nah. You're talking milk and cookies, Fenton. I've got just the right movie for Mary Lou and Glenda." He scanned the shelf of video display boxes directly in front of him, then suddenly reached out and grabbed one. "How's this?" he asked, starting to read the blurb out loud. " 'A group of teenagers trapped in a mall have their arms, legs, and heads chopped off and stuffed into shopping bags by robots that have gone berserk.' Are you guys ready to hear the name of it? It's called . . . *Chopping Mall*!"

Mary Lou clutched my arm and dug her sharp nails

into my flesh. "Aahhh!" she screeched. "Disgustin'."

A thrill of pain ran through me, but I wasn't about to get hysterical like Mary Lou. Roddy and Ethan, meantime, had broken out into hoarse laughter. I could hear echoes of that old braying laugh of Roddy's that used to infuriate me a couple of years back when he was twelve or so.

I guess we were making quite a bit of noise because the next moment I heard footsteps coming toward us. It was probably the manager. Nobody wanted crazy-acting kids in their store. I turned stiffly.

To my relief, it was Patty. I'd almost forgotten about her. She was frowning slightly and looking kind of anxious. Mary Lou gulped and hastily introduced Patty to the new boy.

"Mary Lou!" Patty hissed, giving Ethan a flashing look of interest and tossing off a quick "Hi" aimed at both him and Roddy, "We've got to go. Right now."

"Where are you girls rushing off to?" Roddy wanted to know. I had the same question myself. How come Patty was in such a hurry? Ethan, it seemed to me, was just her type. He was the right height for her, too.

Mary Lou took a step toward Roddy and Ethan, her lips curving into a sly smile. "It's because of Glenda's birthday," she said, hunching one shoulder apologetically.

Patty gave Mary Lou a fierce look. What was going on around here, anyway? Mary Lou wished she could stay. Patty wanted to go. And I was in a state of complete bewilderment.

But before I could open my mouth to say anything, Patty grabbed both Mary Lou's hand and mine and practically yanked us out of Horror and Science Fiction toward the main aisle of the store. Clearly, we were heading for the doorway — and fast.

There was something altogether weird about Patty actually running in the opposite direction from a couple of boys. And, even as she propelled Mary Lou and me along with her small, powerful body, I could hear Mary Lou longingly calling out to the now-invisible Roddy and Ethan, "Bye for now. See you-all later maybe. Hmmmm?"

Chapter 3

The moment we three had lurched out onto the sidewalk in front of the video store, Patty and Mary Lou stuck their hands on their hips and shrilled at me in unison, "Surprise!"

I stood there blinking in the bright October sunlight, trying to figure out what was going on.

The next moment I saw a familiar sight. My mother was standing beside her car — which was double-parked just a short distance from the store entrance — and waving at me frantically. She was dressed in one of her ladies' luncheon outfits, a dressy suit and a silk blouse, and her ash-blonde hair was set and sprayed into sculptured waves that didn't stir in the brisk breeze.

"Glenn-da! Oh, Glenda." My mother was smiling and beckoning me and my friends toward the car. I looked at Patty and Mary Lou, and saw them glance at each other and nod knowingly as they gently urged me forward.

Like the pieces of a puzzle, things started falling into place. Patty had been the lookout. She'd *known* my mother would be coming by for us and had sent me to the back of the video store with Mary Lou until she'd seen my mother drive up. She'd known, too, of course, that my mother would have to double-park on a busy Havenhurst shopping street on a Saturday afternoon. Everything had been prearranged.

But why? Why was my mother here at all?

As soon as we reached the car, my mother planted her plump hands on my shoulders and gave me a big kiss on the cheek. "Happy birthday again, darling. Oh, I'm so glad you wore the locket. It looks lovely. Sit in the front with me, Glenda."

Patty and Mary Lou scrambled into the back seat as my mother started around to the driver's side. I could hear them giggling faintly back there.

"What's going on, anyway?" I asked, turning to look at them before my mother got in the car.

"We already told you," Patty said, her dark eyes dancing. "Surprise."

"This is the surprise?" I whispered. "My mother's going to drive us somewhere?"

As if they'd been programmed, my two friends put their fingers on their lips. At the same moment, my mother got in and slammed the door.

"Where are we going?" I asked her with an air of purest innocence.

My mother's profile was immobile as she maneuvered the car into the stream of Main Street traffic. "Now, Glenda," she said with a very faint smile, "you have to let me hold onto my secret just a little bit longer."

I sat back, trying to resign myself to just wait and see. But I wasn't altogether sure I liked surprises. They could be really embarrassing, especially for somebody in my condition. I was too fat to meet anybody new. And I certainly didn't want to meet anybody "old" who'd known me when I was thinner.

Very soon we'd left the Havenhurst business district and were driving in the direction of the newly-enlarged shopping mall near the edge of town. I was almost sure my mother was going to turn in at the mall and drop us off for lunch and a movie. I kept telling myself that was probably the plan, and I began to relax a little.

But when we came to the mall itself, the entrances just zoomed past us and we kept on going, with the radio lushly tuned in to one of the easy-listening music stations that my mother liked. The music gave everybody an excuse not to have to say anything. I could just imagine, though, what Patty and Mary Lou must have been thinking as they were being drowned by the rear-seat stereo with "Moonlight and Roses" or some such mushy tune.

As for me, I was beginning to have the weirdest feeling. I felt like I was being kidnapped by my own mother.

I twisted uncomfortably in my seat. "I thought you were running a fashion-show luncheon this afternoon," I said to my mother almost accusingly and in a voice loud enough for Patty and Mary Lou to hear. "How come you've got the time to be driving *us* all over the place?"

My mother's frozen smile didn't change as she concentrated on the road ahead. We were now out on one of the main Long Island highways, sailing past industrial parks, shopping centers, and housing developments, all neatly laid out on flat stretches of land that had once been mostly potato fields.

With a shrug, I looked around at Patty and Mary Lou. Mary Lou just shrugged back. But Patty unexpectedly gave me a mischievous wink. Something was up. Definitely, something sneaky had been planned for me. And, short of jumping out of the moving car, I didn't have the slightest chance of escape.

I turned and went back to watching the ribbon of highway unfold before us, while Patty and Mary Lou continued their unnatural silence and my normally talkative mother remained mum. Suddenly, there was a clicking sound. My mother had put on her right blinker and was starting to pull off the main road. Directly ahead, at the end of the exit ramp, rose a large sign with the words HOLIDAY PARK MOTEL and beneath it a slightly smaller one announcing DELUXE ACCOMMODATIONS, SWIMMING POOL AND SAUNA, BANQUET FACILITIES FOR ALL OCCASIONS. Just beyond the signs lay a sweep of artificially green lawn and a sleek, low-lying building with wings that angled off it.

Neatly, my mother berthed the car in a parking space and turned to me with a satisfied sigh. "Well, Glenda dear, here we are at last. I hope you're going to enjoy the little surprise I have in store for you."

"Surprise?" I repeated warily as I reluctantly lumbered out of the car. "B-but I thought I told you . . ."

Patty and Mary Lou had already piled out of the back seat. "Ooh, it's nice here." Mary Lou exclaimed. "What a fancy motel. It looks almost like a . . . country club."

Anxiously, I followed my mother as she confidently led the way into the thickly carpeted lobby. We went down a wide corridor lined with mirrors toward a bunch of signs with arrows on them pointing to BANQUET ROOM A, BANQUET ROOM B, and so on.

My knees had already become wobbly. In fact, I was beginning to feel like I was being hustled off to my own execution. What had my mother gone and done? Why didn't she ever *listen* to me? The last thing in the world I wanted was to enter one of those banquet rooms and find a bunch of screeching kids from school jumping up and down and yelling "Surprise!"

The boys in my class were awful this year, pimply or shrimpy, or both. How could I even *look* at them after Justin? And the girls, on the other hand, all seemed to have become slender and gorgeous, making *me* more self-conscious than ever. Suppose there was dancing? I just couldn't get up on the floor and shake all over like a bowl of quivering jelly. I *wouldn't.*

I fell into step beside Patty. "You knew about this all along, you and Mary Lou. Didn't you?" I whispered.

Patty gave me an almost pitying look. "Oh, for

heaven's sake, Glenda, lighten up, will you? Your mother is only trying . . ."

Patty's words trailed off. My mother had come to a sudden halt at the entrance to a large room filled with round tables arranged on either side of a raised walkway. Pale pink cloths and matching napkins folded in fancy shapes covered the tables. The room was shrill with the sound of chattering women, all of them about my mother's age. Some of the ladies were already seated at the tables, while others were standing around in gossipy clusters. There wasn't a man or boy in sight *or* anybody in their teens like Patty, Mary Lou, and me.

My mother turned and beamed at us triumphantly. "Well, this is it, girls. It's my annual women's club fall-fashion-show luncheon. And I thought to myself that, well, since Glenda kept insisting she didn't want a regular birthday party this year, I'd just set up a little birthday-luncheon table *here* for her and a few friends."

With that, my mother charged into the room, greeting people to her left and right, and leading us to my special "birthday" table.

I found myself shaking with relief and blushing with embarrassment at the same time. At least it wasn't going to be some terrible teen party to which my mother, not knowing whom to ask, had simply invited the entire ninth grade.

On the other hand, what was I doing at one of those creamed-chicken lunches for mostly overweight ladies, with a fashion show thrown in to display clothes that only looked good on toothpick-shaped models? And what did my friends *really* think of this "surprise" my mother had cooked up? Why couldn't the three of us simply have had lunch at the Burger Barn or the Pizza Pan over at the mall?

The table toward which we were heading was alongside the fashion-show runway. It was set for four, and there was already somebody seated at it. I figured she was one of my mother's friends — and certainly the fattest of them — as she rose with a jolly smile to greet us.

"Ah, Giselle," my mother exclaimed, rushing around the table to embrace the person who was standing there. "How wonderful that you got here early. Let me introduce you to the other girls."

I gasped inwardly. *Other* girls? What did my mother mean by that? I exchanged rapid glances with Patty and Mary Lou, and could see they were as baffled as I was. But my mother was already making the introductions. "Giselle, this is Patty. Giselle, this is Mary Lou. Giselle, this is Glenda. Girls, this is Giselle Wappington."

We three stood there grinning sheepishly and silently begging for an explanation. Because it was pretty clear after a closer look that Giselle *was* our age.

"I decided Giselle just *had* to be part of Glenda's birthday surprise," my mother went on enthusiastically, "because, you see, she's just moved to town. And she'll be attending Havenhurst Junior High with you girls. So this is the perfect occasion for all of you to get acquainted."

By now Giselle had leaned forward and started to shake hands with each of us, burbling in a pleasantly throaty voice, "I'm *so* glad to meet you all."

Hmm. Fourteen going on forty-five, I thought to myself—and probably so did my friends. Then, almost cautiously, we all took our seats.

By now, I'd been able to really study Giselle's appearance—her rosy, full moon of a face, partly framed by close-cropped dark-brown hair, her twinkly eyes nearly confined to slits by the flesh surrounding them, her bulging cheeks and bouncing chins. What, I began to wonder, did my mother really have in mind in inviting her here today?

Was Giselle, as a very, very fat person, supposed to be some kind of warning to me of what I might become if I kept on mooning over my fading summer romance with Justin? As for my friends, what did they secretly think of of my mother just plopping Giselle down among us? And what did Giselle herself think? How did she feel about being Exhibit A at my birthday lunch? Or didn't she see it that way?

My mother was fussing happily now with the extra-large flower arrangement in the center of the table. She turned it toward me so that I could read the glossy ribbon around the bouquet that spelled out in silvery sparkles the words *Happy Birthday, Glenda!*

Seeing the genuine pleasure in my mother's eyes, I

managed a bright but somewhat toothy smile, sat back in my chair, and took a deep breath. Maybe, I told myself, the thing to do was to stop being so touchy and "lighten up," as Patty had suggested. After all, my mother *was* trying in her own way to make things nice for me. And there was one more thing I guessed I should have been grateful to her for. By inviting Giselle Wappington to join us, my mother had saved me from being the fattest person at my fourteenth birthday party.

Chapter 4

The fruit cup was already on the table. For a few moments, we all stared down at our plates in silent embarrassment. Then Giselle broke the ice by giving each of us a friendly glance and digging into hers. Eating, after all, was something most people had in common. Except, of course, for Mary Lou, who tried to do as little of it as possible.

"So," Patty ventured politely as she slowly aimed her spoon toward the small crystal dish in front of her, "you've, um, just moved to Havenhurst, Giselle."

Giselle very daintily finished conveying a piece of grapefruit to her lips, "Um-hmmm," she replied. "I guess you could say I'm the new girl in town. Think I'll like it here?"

I shuddered inwardly. Being fat in Havenhurst was about the worst thing I could think of. And who knew that better than I? Only last year I'd been the eighth-grade monstrosity of Havenhurst Junior High. And the way things had been going this fall, I was rapidly qualifying for ninth.

"Where did you-all live before?" Mary Lou inquired

softly, a piece of pineapple dangling off the edge of her spoon.

"In the city," Giselle replied, her full cheeks beaming pinkly.

"New *York* City?" Mary Lou raised her eyebrows in dismay. "That's so far away."

"What makes you say that?" asked Giselle. "It's just a train ride from here to there."

Patty gave Mary Lou a slightly withering look. "*She* almost never goes into Manhattan. Well, I guess most of us out here don't." Patty lowered her eyes. "We're probably going to seem like a real bunch of hicks to you."

"Oh, I don't think so," Giselle answered as she efficiently polished off her fruit cup. "I'd be happy to show you girls around town anytime. Lived there most of my life."

"What kind of a school did you go to?" I asked. This had been my first chance to get in a question to Giselle.

"It was a private school . . . all girls." Giselle nodded with apparent pleasure at the memory. "We really had a ball."

I wanted to hear more about a school where fat girls could be so happy. Maybe, I reflected, big-city people were more accepting of the wide variety of shapes and sizes that human beings came in. Or maybe Giselle was just so self-confident and likeable that nothing and nobody ever made her feel bad.

But before I could find out any more, Mary Lou

suddenly looked up and exclaimed, "Ooh, here they come! The models. Look, everybody."

Three sleek young women were now swirling and swishing their way toward us along the runway. They were wearing smart-looking heavy tweeds, boots that wouldn't have zipped up over my forearms, and bizarre broad-brimmed hats that would have made somebody like me look like a teapot — a very large teapot, of course.

"Ooh, stunning," Mary Lou commented after we'd listened to the announcer's description of the clothes and been told the names of the designers and the stores where they could be bought. Of course, Mary Lou could afford to say "stunning." She had the same kind of sticklike body as those models, except she didn't quite know how to use hers yet.

Patty shook her head from side to side in disagreement. "Those clothes are altogether too bulky," she pronounced. "I couldn't carry such big hairy tweeds. What are short people supposed to do?"

I nodded in sympathy as the mannequins began to drift off, because even though I wasn't short like Patty, I had my own figure problems. "Aren't those models exactly the kind of people you love to hate?" I murmured to the table in general. But I especially wondered what Giselle would have to say.

She'd been watching the last model disappear off the runway and turned to me with a blissful smile. "Great clothes," she chanted. "I just *love* going to fashion shows."

I exchanged an astonished look with Patty. How could somebody who must have had to clothes shop at the nearest tentmaker's "love" going to fashion shows? For me, watching thin people cavorting in clothes that I couldn't wear was one of the worst forms of torture.

Giselle must have caught my silent exchange with Patty. "Modeling clothes is practically in my blood," she added by way of explanation. "See, I used to *be* a fashion model."

All three of our mouths must have fallen open at once. Giselle, on the other hand, was already delicately stuffing hers with the tossed salad drowned in creamy crumbles of blue cheese that sat beside her dinner plate.

"Oh?" Patty finally managed, barely disguising her disbelief.

Giselle broke a soft roll in half and buttered it. "Yup, I was a child fashion model until I was eight." She grinned. "For chubby sizes. And before that I was a toddler model. And before that a baby model. All fatties, of course."

"Of course," I murmured before I even realized I was speaking out loud.

But Giselle merely threw me an understanding look. "So I know a whole lot about modeling. I'll show you my publicity photos sometime if you're interested."

I nodded to show eagerness. But what I really wanted to ask Giselle was what she was in training for now. From the way she looked *and* the way she was eating, the only thing I could think of was a "fat-lady-in-the-circus" model.

It was a relief when Patty quickly changed the subject, inquiring how come Giselle's family had moved out of the city. And we learned that it was on account of her father having relocated his electronics business to somewhere on Long Island.

Then, right after that, the waitresses brought our main course — a naked baked chicken breast for me (my mother had ordered me the "lean cuisine" luncheon) and something sizzling, golden, and buttery for Patty, Mary Lou, and Giselle. At that moment, the models came back. This time they did the "casual clothing" scene in clinging pants, miniskirts, short-shorts, tights, and other skimpy unwearables.

Finally, dessert arrived — chocolate whipped-cream parfaits for *them* and a watery lemon ice for *me*. And, just as a parting jab, the models made their last appearance in snaky-looking, low-cut evening gowns. This time they sashayed off the runway and glided among the tables. They actually went around ours twice. I was sure they did it out of pure spite. But Giselle just beamed at them in her usual way.

Then suddenly my mother was at my side with a birthday cake lit with glowing candles and everyone was singing "Happy Birthday." Eyes tightly closed — and wishing my secret wish about Justin — I bent to my huffing and puffing.

My mother kissed me and went back to her own

table. Cake knife in hand, I gazed at the creamy delight in front of me. It definitely wasn't "lean cuisine." In fact, it was probably the only yummy thing I'd get to eat today.

But before I could slice into it, two small packages appeared on the table and Mary Lou shrieked, "Now, now! Open your presents now, Glenda. I just can't wait to see what you'll think about what Patty and I got you."

I hesitated a moment and then reached for the squarish, boxy package wrapped in elegant flowered paper.

"Oh," Mary Lou said, slightly crestfallen, "that one's not ours. Patty and I went halves on your present. That one must be from Giselle."

I turned to Giselle in surprise. She didn't even know me and yet she'd brought me a gift. "You didn't have to . . ." I started to stammer.

Giselle merely shook her head, her eyes twinkling.

Anxiously, I tore at the flowered paper. What had Giselle gotten me? It would be really embarrassing if it was anything too expensive.

The wrapping was off now, and I carefully lifted the lid of the box.

"Oh," I gasped with relief. "*Pretty* notepaper. I can really use this. Thank you, Giselle. Thanks very much."

I passed the box of stationery around to show Patty and Mary Lou. The sheets were decorated in a sophisticated pattern, not the usual loopy teen stuff. The pages might be a little small for one of my really long letters to Sara in California. But they'd be perfect for — *if*, that is — I ever did find myself writing to . . . Justin.

So far so good. Presents — the wrong kind — could get me awfully upset. The other present lying on the table, the one from Patty and Mary Lou, was in a long, slim, gold box. I'd once gotten a gift certificate for a mini membership at a reducing salon in a box like that. It had made me feel, well . . . fat.

Gingerly, I lifted the lid. Sure enough it *was* some kind of a certificate. But I couldn't read it because it was upside down.

"Well? Well?" Mary Lou was gasping anxiously, as I slowly turned the box around. "Do you like it, Glenda? It's a lifetime membership to the new video store plus *thirty* free rentals. That's why we stopped there today. So Patty could buy it. Wasn't that clever of us?"

My eyes were sliding down the fine print on the certificate listing the whole bunch of things a membership entitled you to — discounts on all rentals, no deposit required, rent a movie on Saturday and get one for Sunday free, rent two on Tuesday and get a third one free, no extra charge for rewinding tapes, and so on and so on.

I looked up, still digesting all the advantages of being a lifetime member at the video store. Silently, I wondered, "Whose lifetime? Theirs or mine?" Out loud, I stammered, "Oh-h-h. This is *great*, Patty and Mary Lou."

"Do you really like it, Glenda?" Patty asked earnestly, her dark eyes searching my face. "I figured you'd enjoy having your very own membership. You can even call up and reserve any tape you want if you're a member."

"And they'll deliver it free," Mary Lou chirped. "If it was bad weather or something, you wouldn't *even* have to go out."

I nodded as enthusiastically as I could. But words just wouldn't come to me. Maybe I was taking my birthday present from my friends the wrong way. But I was getting this sort of dreary picture of myself spending the entire winter roosting in front of the TV like an oversize hen. Was that how Patty and Mary Lou saw me in their secret thoughts?

Giselle, sitting on my right, had eagerly leaned over and was reading my new gift certificate. "This is super," she declared. "Sounds like a much better membership deal than the video stores in my old neighborhood used to give." Her plump fingers, surprisingly dainty at the tips, came to rest on my sleeve, and she gazed into my eyes with a yearning smile.

"Maybe," she added, "you'll invite me over sometime to watch with you, Glenda."

I gulped and hastily nodded. The image I'd just had of myself as a blob in front of the TV set intensified. Now there were two of us — Giselle Wappington, the fattest girl in Havenhurst, and me, her close second.

All at once, an awful feeling came over me. Just like the minimembership I'd once gotten to the reducing salon, my birthday present from Mary Lou and Patty had made me feel totally depressed.

Chapter 5

"A fashion model," Patty remarked, making a sharp, clicking sound with her tongue. "Just think of *her* being a fashion model."

It was Monday, two days after my birthday, and Patty, Mary Lou, and I were sitting in third-period study hall whispering to one another.

I gave Patty a defensive look. "She *said* she was a 'fat' model. For chubby kids. There are even fatties who model clothes for grown-ups. So why can't you believe her?"

"Sshh!" Mary Lou hissed. "She might walk in here any minute."

"*If* she gets into our ninth-grade homeroom program," Patty reminded her. Today was the day Giselle Wappington was registering at Havenhurst Junior High and hoping to be in the same class as we three.

Patty turned to me. "How did your mother ever *find* Giselle in the first place, Glenda?" She paused to snicker at her own words. "Well, I realize she'd be big enough to see from pretty far off. But you know what I mean."

I was surprised at how hostile Patty sounded toward Giselle this morning. She'd been polite enough to her on Saturday.

"Oh," I explained briefly, "I found out it was through my mother's friend, Evelyn Bagley, the real estate lady. She sold the Wappingtons their house and told my mother they had this teenage daughter, an only child just like me, and so on."

Patty nodded guardedly. "I see." She paused a moment. "So what are you planning to do about Giselle, Glenda?"

I looked around in alarm. "Do? Me?" Both girls stared at me blankly. "Why me?" I inquired in a baffled tone. "Why not 'us'?"

Patty leaned forward. "Because it's already pretty clear she's going to glue herself to you. And if you let her . . . Well, let's face it. It's not going to be too great for your image."

I sat up a little straighter. It was just possible that Patty was right about the burden of Giselle Wappington falling on me. As if I didn't have enough troubles.

I could see, too, what Patty meant about my "image." Being pals with the fattest girl in school wasn't exactly the road to popularity. On the other hand, *I'd* once been the fattest girl in school and I knew how lonely and miserable that could be. So would it really hurt if we were nice to Giselle, at least until she got settled and maybe made some other friends?

Besides, I was interested in Giselle as another fat

person. Why did she eat so much? Didn't she care about how she looked? Was she really as happy-go-lucky as she seemed?

"Aren't you being just a little bit mean about Giselle?" I challenged Patty.

"Meow, meow," Mary Lou broke in softly. "Why don't we all quiet down and study some? We're gettin' looks from the teacher."

I opened my science notebook and let the cover flop over with a thud. "Don't blame me," I whispered. "I'm not the one who's being catty."

When I glanced up, I caught a burning look in Patty's dark eyes. It was hard to tell what was really bothering her. Could she actually have been jealous of the fact that Giselle had once been a model — even a fat one — and she never had?

The next period was lunch. As soon as we got to the cafeteria, Mary Lou and Patty parked their belongings with me at our regular table and set off for the hot-food line.

I looked longingly in their direction. How delicious all those horrible steam-table smells were to me — oniony burgers, greasy fries, cheesy macaroni, mashed potatoes puddled with gloppy brown gravy.

Slowly, I began to unwrap the tasteless, odorless, low-low-low-calorie lunch I'd brought from home — a small container of plain, no-fat yogurt, a clump of alfalfa sprouts, and some cucumbers. I was fooling myself, of course. By three o'clock my stomach would be howling. And the minute I got home from school, I'd be secretly stuffing my face with crispy, crunchy, high-calorie snacks.

Suddenly, another deliciously tempting smell hit my nostrils. This time it was the aroma of tuna-noodle surprise, one of the regular Monday specials — yucky to some but not to me. Its faint fishiness was definitely wafting my way. I could almost taste the crispy browned noodles on top and the lumpy white sauce flaked with tuna inside. Was I hallucinating? Where was that smell coming from? Why was it so powerful?

I lifted my head and turned it slightly to the side, nostrils still quivering.

"Ah, *there* you are, Glenda," a throaty voice said just behind my ear. "I figured I'd find you in lunch period."

Two plump hands set a well-filled food tray down beside me. It contained a couple of hot muffins slathered with melting margarine, a double side order of french fries, vanilla creme pudding, and, of course, the tuna-noodle surprise that I'd been inhaling.

The next moment Giselle Wappington herself slid gracefully onto the bench and settled herself next to me.

"Well," she puffed with a jolly air, "I guess I made it."

"You mean you, um, got registered and . . . everything?" I realized I didn't sound too friendly or welcoming, but my mind was on Patty and Mary Lou, who would soon be coming back to the table.

"You bet I got registered." Giselle leaned happily toward her food. "And, Glenda, the people in the principal's office were *so* nice. It took a little urging on my part. But I finally got exactly what I wanted."

"Exactly?" I echoed.

"Exactly. I told them I wanted to be in the same class with *you*. And your friends. At first they said 'impossible.' Because your ninth-grade homeroom was more crowded than any of the others. But," Giselle gurgled, "I can be *very* persuasive. I pointed out one thing and another about why that was the best program for me. And . . . voilà. Here I am!"

"*That's* great," I said, trying hard to show enthusiasm. "Patty and Mary Lou will be glad to hear it, too. They should be back any minute."

Of course, I was lying through my teeth. Patty hadn't exactly taken Giselle to her heart as a fourth member of our little group. Nor did she want to see her cozying up to me, although I still wasn't sure what her reasons were.

I sat staring thoughtfully at my yogurt for a few moments. Giselle followed my gaze, giving my lunch a quick once-over.

Her eyes opened the widest I'd ever seen them. "Is that all you're going to eat, Glenda?"

This was the first time the subject of food had come up between us. I nodded. "It's all I'm going to *try* to eat. I have to take off eleven and a half pounds. And don't talk to me about exercise. That only makes me eat more."

Giselle gave me a curious look. "Eleven and a half pounds. Exactly?"

"Yes. Because that's what I've gained since the end of summer. You wouldn't believe it now. But I looked just about perfect last summer." I paused wistfully. "I went out with a terrific boy. Everything was . . . different."

Giselle leaned closer. "Really? Tell me about it."

I backed away slightly. "There's nothing to tell," I said. "He lives out of town and he doesn't write or phone. I haven't seen him or heard from him since the end of August."

"Why? Because you're fat?"

"No. He doesn't know I'm fat." Giselle's question had baffled me for a moment. "Don't you understand?" I said, sounding a little impatient. "I'm fat *because* he doesn't write or phone."

Giselle's face looked like a balloon getting ready to burst. And then suddenly it did. Her cheeks swelled, her eyes became disappearing slits, and laughter sputtered from her lips.

"So, Glenda," she said, trying to choke back her merriment, "what's the *difference* if you're fat or thin? It isn't as though he's not writing to 'fat' Glenda. He isn't even writing to 'thin' Glenda. You could lose *twenty* pounds, and still he wouldn't write. Are you sure this boy is worth agonizing over?"

I had actually found myself smiling faintly along with Giselle's laughter. Her reasoning, I had to admit, was pretty sound. But soon I was stirring my yogurt morosely again. "You don't understand," I murmured. "It's the . . . frustration. I thought Justin really cared. Now I'm thinking maybe I was too fat for him even when I was thin. . . ."

Giselle, who had been gobbling up her lunch, placed a hand on my arm.

"Listen, would you believe me if I told you there was more to life than starving yourself to death and being ignored by boys with short-term memories? Anyhow, a little while ago you said you looked 'perfect' last summer. But you know what? I think you look 'perfect' right now."

"Hmmm," I mumbled. " 'Perfect' for what?"

Giselle threw me a challenging look. "For what? I'll tell you for what. What would you say if I told you that you were the perfect size and shape and had just the right looks for a teen fashion model? Huh?"

I stared at Giselle in disbelief. "Modeling? Me?" Scenes of last Saturday's fashion show flashed through my mind. "You've got to be kidding."

"Uh-uh," Giselle said, her mouth rather full at the moment. "Why does everybody always think of models as having to be skinny-skinny? I already told you about me. I could have gone on from modeling chubby children's clothes into plus-size teen fashions except that, well, I got a little *too* overweight. But you, Glenda . . . you'd be just right."

I dipped into my cup of yogurt, its tangy nothingness slipping effortlessly down my throat. A flutter of excitement had started to ripple through me. "You mean *I* could be a model for, um, fat-teen fashions?"

Giselle was rapidly polishing off her vanilla creme pudding. "Right," she nodded. "See, to model clothes even for real fatties, you mustn't be *too* fat. What you've got to be is padded just enough all over and well proportioned. And pretty in a wholesome way." Giselle paused. "Like I said, you're exactly what some of the modeling agencies could be looking for. I used to get most of my jobs through one that specialized in chubby kids. It was called All-Girl Models."

Hungry for more information, I watched as Giselle deftly cleaned the sides of her pudding dish with her spoon. "And I do know about modeling, Glenda. So I could give you all sorts of tips — "

Silently, I waited for Giselle to go on. But, just when I was getting almost unbearably interested, she had suddenly stopped talking. Her attention seemed to have been caught by something that was taking place a few tables away from us.

I followed the direction in which Giselle was looking, and there, sure enough, were Patty and Mary Lou. They had set their food trays down temporarily at a table full of kids from our class. Neither Giselle nor I, of course, could hear what they were saying through the din of the cafeteria. But, from their gestures, I sensed immediately that they must have spotted Giselle at the table with me. And they were talking about her.

I could see Patty spread her hands far apart. Was she describing Giselle's size? I could see Mary Lou clap her palms to her cheeks. Was she shaking her head woefully in mock sympathy? I could see the sly grins on the faces of the kids my two friends were talking to.

There had been so many times when *I* had looked up suddenly to find kids gathered in groups that were gossiping about *me*. Did Giselle suspect they were talking about her? It was hard to tell. Her lips were still smiling. But it seemed to me that her face was clouded. I'd never seen it that way.

I squeezed her arm tightly, hoping to distract her. "I'm glad you got into our class, Giselle," I said, this time with sincerity. "I think you're really going to like it here in Havenhurst, too, once you get used to it. It just takes time."

Giselle turned to me. Maybe I was wrong about her losing her cool. Her full lips were still pursed into that smile and, in gently even tones, she murmured, "I know."

Chapter 6

All-Girl Models! Since Monday, when Giselle Wappington had first mentioned the New York City modeling agency to me, I'd hardly been able to think about anything else. Even my more-or-less-dead hopes of ever hearing from Justin didn't seem to come to mind as often as before.

Perfect, Giselle had said. My present weight was perfect. And so were my proportions. Then the very next day, when we'd talked again, Giselle had told me that she'd found out the All-Girl agency was still in business and still having "open-call" interviews for young people who wanted to apply as models. Open call, Giselle explained, meant that the agency would see you without an appointment if you came in at a certain time. In the case of All-Girl Models, which dealt mainly with school kids, it was any Saturday morning between nine-thirty and noon.

I could see that Giselle knew what she was talking about. I had a whole lot of confidence in her. *And* a Saturday was coming along in just a couple more days. So what was stopping me?

The thing that was stopping me was that I hadn't

said a single word about Giselle's idea to my mother yet. During the early part of the week, she'd been busy almost every evening. But now, at last, on Thursday, my mother and father and I were about to sit down to a cozy family meal. It was my big chance to bring up Giselle's suggestion that she and I take the train into Manhattan on Saturday.

The first part of our little family discussion went smoothly enough. My mother even knew all about Giselle's having once been a baby and child model.

"News travels fast in Havenhurst," she assured me, working energetically on her first-course salad. My mother's latest dieting idea was to start out by stuffing herself with a bulky serving of raw vegetation in order to reduce her appetite for the rest of the meal. My father, who ate only cooked vegetables — and mighty few of those — was contentedly spooning up his soup.

I poked around among the salad greens on my plate. It was always a delicate operation getting my mother to agree to anything the slightest bit out of the ordinary that I wanted to do. So I knew I had to proceed carefully. When I got to the part about Giselle saying I had good qualifications to be a plus-teen model and that she even knew the right agency to apply to, I broke out into a sweat even though it was a chilly October evening.

Amazingly, my mother put down her fork and stopped chewing. "Really?" she said, her eyes widening. I could almost see the little trains of thought racing around faster and faster in her mind. "Are you actually saying, Glenda, that Giselle Wappington has some kind of an 'in' with one of the big modeling agencies?"

Since Giselle had stopped modeling about six years ago, I didn't really know if she had an "in" anymore. So I just let that part of my mother's question go. Nor did I honestly know how big the All-Girl agency was. It was probably just a pipsqueak among the real biggies that created all those famous cover girls and glamorous fashion models who got to be household names. But in the sense that it was an agency that supplied plump babies, chubby toddlers, and oversize teens, I felt it was safe to nod and say yes it was "big."

My mother actually moved her chair back a few inches from the table. She glanced toward my father. "What do you think of that, Harold? This interesting family from the city moves into Havenhurst. I introduce their one and only daughter to Glenda. And it turns out she has a background in modeling and she offers our little girl a chance to get started on, of all things, a modeling career of her own."

My father, who always acted like he hadn't been tuned into the conversation until he was asked a direct question, gave my mother a look of pure bafflement.

"What's that you're saying, Grace? Glenda, a model? You can't be serious. Do you really think that's something for her?"

It seemed my father must have missed the point about the *kind* of model I was hoping to be. So I launched into a repeat description of how the All-Girl agency supplied models for chubby-size fashions and how I had a special advantage because my present weight was just right for showing off clothing for plump teens.

But that didn't seem to get through to him either. He put down his spoon, wiped his mouth with his napkin, and began shaking his head back and forth. "I can't believe you mean it, Grace," he said to my mother. "Every intelligent person knows the modeling game is nothing but a racket. It's a rip-off for naive females. They spend a fortune trying to break in and end up disappointed and broke besides. Don't you think I get around the city enough? I see what goes on."

Compared to my mother, my father did spend more time in Manhattan since his accounting practice took him to a lot of business firms that were located there. But just the same, I could practically *see* my mother's hackles rise. My father had actually attacked her intelligence as well as females in general.

My mother's baby-blue eyes grew icy with indignation. "Well, I never . . ." She paused to take a deep breath. "You talk as though I were some stupid little suburban housewife, Harold. I've been running clubs and organizing functions most of my life. I . . . I . . ."

My father was already backing down and waving his hands at my mother to try to calm her. The light was bouncing off his glasses, and his moustache was twitching slightly. Even though he definitely didn't seem to be on my side, I couldn't help feeling a little bit sorry for him.

"All I'm saying, Grace," he mumbled half apologetically, "is that you've got to be careful about getting involved with some kind of slick outfit that'll put you to a lot of expense and make all sorts of promises. . . ."

I didn't like the way the conversation was going. "But it isn't like that at all," I broke in, worried that my father was beginning to give my mother too many wrong ideas. "Giselle *knows* the All-Girl agency. She got most of her baby and toddler and chubby little girl modeling jobs through them." I gave my parents an intense look. "Honestly. You can ask her."

My mother had begun to relax slightly. "Well, naturally, I will. And I'll check all this out with Giselle's parents as well." She turned to my father. "I don't know what made you think, Harold, that I'd just go stumbling into this blindly. I've got my eyes open all the time, believe me."

As my mother went on reassuring my father that her guard was up, I began to feel more and more uneasy. "But," I added hopefully, "if it all checks out — and I'm sure it will — it'll be okay for Giselle and me to go into the city on Saturday morning for an interview. Right?"

My mother's brow wrinkled slightly. "*This* Saturday? Oh, I'm afraid not."

"Why?" I asked anxiously. "Saturday mornings. From nine-thirty to twelve. That's when they see people without an appointment. What's the sense of waiting?"

My mother was smiling again as she rose from the

table to take away the salad and soup plates. "It can't be this Saturday, Glenda, because I have an all-day meeting. It'll probably have to be the one after. . . ."

I pushed back my chair and stood up, too. "What's that got to do with —" I stopped myself abruptly because already the horrible truth had dawned on me. "You're not planning to go *with* us?" My mother's back was already turned. I followed her into the kitchen. "Because you absolutely don't need to. Giselle knows how to get there and what to say and everything," I explained urgently.

I dashed around to the other side of the sink. "Except for really little kids," I went on, "the agencies don't even like it if your mother comes with you on your first interview. In fact, they actually *hate* mothers who tag along. They call them 'stage mamas.' "

"Now, Glenda," my mother said, taking our main course of baked fish out of the oven, "calm down. You heard what your father had to say. And I really do think he has a point. It just isn't right for a fourteen-year-old girl to go all by herself to apply for a modeling job."

"But I wouldn't *be* all by myself." I could hear the first note of hysteria creeping into my voice. I knew I had come up against a stone wall. But something in me refused to give up. "You're spoiling everything for me," I shrilled. "You know how miserable I've been these last months about getting fat again. And now for the first time in my life I find out there might actually be something *good* about being fifteen or twenty pounds overweight. Something that would make me feel it wasn't all *bad* to . . . to . . ."

"You're not *that* many pounds overweight," my mother corrected me as she arranged the food on a warm platter. "And you wouldn't be overweight at all if you'd stop mooning over that boy from last summer. One of these days you'll get it through your head that he was just a summer romance. And it's over. It happens all the time."

Even though my mother was probably right, her words about Justin really hurt. I'd spent so much time wondering if he'd ever really liked me at all and feeling so . . . rejected. I followed her back to the table with tears blurring my eyes.

"Harold," my mother said, setting the food down in front of my father, "please tell your daughter that she's not 'fat.' She always exaggerates. Now she's talking like she's some kind of a monstrosity and if she doesn't get that modeling job it's going to be the end of the world."

I remained beside my chair, refusing to sit down. "Well, you're right, it is! Don't you see, if I could get into modeling, even for plump teens, I'd feel a million times better about myself. How fat do I have to be," I growled at my mother, "for you to admit I'm fat? As fat as Giselle Wappington?"

My father was looking bewildered again. "What now?" he inquired. "I don't understand what this is all about. I thought it was all settled that your mother would go into the city with you and look over this so-called modeling agency when she has a chance."

I picked up my chair and banged it down on the floor with a thud to show how angry I was getting. But my father was determined to have the rest of his say.

"As for who's fat and who isn't fat," he went on, "I'm tired of hearing that argument over and over again in this house. I'm tired, too, of hearing about that boy from last summer, whatever his name was. I don't approve of a mere child like Glenda having a steady boyfriend. And I'm tired of hearing you two bicker every time the three of us sit down together. When is all this going to stop?"

"Stop?" I exclaimed in a rising screech. "Stop? Let me tell you, it's only just starting. Because I'm not a 'mere child.' I'm fourteen. And if I say I'm fat, I'm fat. So you can both of you just quit trying to interfere in my life. From now on, I'm going to solve my problems in my own way!"

The next moment I went rushing off to my room. A series of skirmishes, or even a pitched battle, with my mother over our everyday disagreements was one thing. But this time my usually mild-mannered father had gotten into the act as well. And *that* was too much for me.

Chapter 7

It was Saturday afternoon at the end of a week in which nearly everything had gone wrong. So wrong, in fact, that I found myself wandering all alone over to the video store to use the membership Patty and Mary Lou had given me for my birthday.

Everybody seemed to be giving me lots of space today. My mother, of course, was off at her all-day meeting — and she and I were hardly talking to each other, anyway. Patty and Mary Lou had been acting cool toward me ever since Giselle had turned up in our ninth-grade homeroom last Monday — as if that was *my* fault. And Giselle herself had gone into New York City on the train without me, after I'd told her I couldn't go along because of the fight with my parents.

I didn't exactly blame Giselle. She had old friends in the city she wanted to see. And I knew the first week at Havenhurst Junior High hadn't been easy for her. Just as I'd secretly predicted, kids had *really* stared at her as she'd made her way through the corridors. And I'd heard them whispering some pretty mean descriptions of her in class, ranging all the way from "wide load" to "balloon trip."

I approached the video rental store without any particular movie in mind. All I wanted was something to feel sorry for myself with. My parents were going to be out for the evening, and I'd be spending a Saturday night alone in front of the TV. An old Bette Davis tearjerker might be nice. Or maybe a gentle Ingrid Bergman mystery-romance. I knew that I didn't want to check out anything in the way of a breezy, up-to-the-minute teen comedy. Because I just didn't feel in the mood to try to relate to kids my own age.

Even going inside the video store, once I got there, seemed to be a chore. So I was standing for a while just peering in the window when suddenly the door opened and a tall figure strode out, nearly bumping my shoulder. I looked up, slightly annoyed, and there was Roddy Fenton. He was carrying a small plastic bag, probably his horror-movie videos for the weekend.

I half expected to see his friend Ethan, from last Saturday, with him. But he seemed to be alone.

"Gosh! Glenda." Roddy acted genuinely surprised. His voice was crackly.

"Um, Roddy," I murmured. It was almost the same time of day that Mary Lou and I had run into him in the store last week.

A few seconds of awkward silence passed between us. "So," Roddy said at last with a crooked grin, "how did your birthday turn out? We never did get together later that day, did we?"

I looked at him blankly. "Were we supposed to?"

Roddy nodded his head jerkily. "Well, your girlfriend seemed to think so."

I remembered Mary Lou being coquettish in the Horror and Science Fiction section of the video store with Ethan and Roddy. "Oh, Mary Lou," I sighed. "She's, um, like that lately." I didn't feel I could say anything more without sounding catty.

Roddy cleared his throat. "Well, anyway, what's happening? You in a rush? Waiting for someone?"

I looked up and down the street for no particular reason. "Uh-uh," I said. "I guess I'm just sort of . . . browsing."

I'd known Roddy for such a long time that I felt I could be honest with him. I was feeling fat, lonely, and discouraged today. And I didn't care if he knew it.

Roddy shifted his plastic bag to his other hand. "Okay," he said a little tentatively. "So why don't we go down to the fast-food joint and let me buy you a Coke? We'll drink to your turning 'sweet fourteen.' "

I raised my eyebrows in surprise. Roddy had remembered Mary Lou's little play on words.

At the burger place, we parked ourselves at a table by the window, and Roddy went off to get the food. "A *diet* Coke," I reminded him, calling over his shoulder as he bounded away. Roddy really had gotten taller and better looking this past year. And he didn't wear glasses anymore. I wondered if his eyesight had improved or he'd started wearing contacts.

Pretty soon he was back with two Cokes plus a hamburger and some fries for himself. Roddy unwrapped the burger and extended it toward me. "Here," he said chummily, "take a bite."

I backed away instinctively because it did smell good and I'd already had my lunch — such as it was — at home. "No thanks," I said firmly. "I have to be careful."

Roddy stared at me across the table. "Of what?"

"Of calories," I replied almost indignantly. "You had plenty to say about how fat I was in the old days when you used to call me 'Jelly Belly.' Or have you forgotten all that?"

Roddy snickered softly, shaking his head back and forth. "Yeah. You *were* a fat kid, Glenda. But you grew out of it."

"Grew *out* of it? I guess you didn't notice how much thinner I was last June than I am now. And," I added sadly, "I managed to stay that way all summer. . . ."

Roddy waved his hand at me. "Girls," he said in a croaky voice. "You're all the same. Always complaining. Nothing's ever right. You know what 'fat' is, Glenda? 'Fat' is like the way you *used* to be. 'Fat' is . . ." he hesitated, "like that new girl at school, the blubber queen, the one I saw you with one day last week. What's her name, anyway?"

"Giselle," I said softly, ". . . Wappington."

"Wappington!" Roddy roared and banged the table a couple of times with his fist. "It fits. It fits. Now *that's* fat. Whew!"

For a few seconds, there he was again, the old Roddy, the one who used to torment *me*. Maybe I'd never been quite as fat as Giselle. But I'd known what it was like to be the object of every sly remark and outright guffaw.

"See," I said to Roddy in a serious tone of voice, "that's the way people act toward you if you look freaky to them. As for me, all you're really saying is that next to Giselle I don't look that fat. But it still doesn't make me feel good about all the weight I've gained since the summer ended."

Roddy lowered his head and dunked a couple of fries in ketchup. I wondered if I'd made him feel ashamed. But actually his mind seemed to have jumped to something else. "Hey, Glenda." He looked up for just a moment, then went quickly back to his dunking. "Talking about last summer, did you ever get that letter I wrote you from camp?"

Roddy's question startled me. But I did clearly recall that letter, his penciled, chicken-scratch handwriting on the envelope and all that boring, impersonal stuff he'd typed inside, describing the computer programs he was working on at camp. The letter had come on a bad day, when things weren't going smoothly with Justin, and I'd tucked it away somewhere and forgotten about it.

"Of course I got your letter," I replied slowly.

Roddy polished off the last of the french fries and looked up. "Guess I forgot to give you my address at camp."

"No, you didn't," I told him. It was odd how I

could still see that envelope, even the return address scribbled in the upper-left-hand corner.

Roddy was slowly tracing a path with his finger through the remaining ketchup on his plate. I wished he'd stop. "So how come you never answered?"

"Answered?" I could feel a tiny jolt inside me. "Was I supposed to?" I asked stupidly.

Roddy jerked his head. It was an old stiff-necked gesture of his. "Would have been nice," he said in a faintly sarcastic tone.

I gasped. "I never really thought —" I stopped myself. "I'm sorry, Roddy." I leaned partway across the table. "See, it came at a time when . . . I was very busy. You know, they worked us all pretty hard at the inn."

But what was the use of my rambling on with empty excuses? Roddy had hoped for an answer, and I hadn't sent him one. How could I tell him that it hadn't even occurred to me at the time to write back?

I turned to look out the window. I guess I'd hurt Roddy's feelings by not writing and it had been on his mind for months now. I'd never even stopped to think — during all this time that *I'd* been hoping to hear from Justin — that a boy could feel rejected, too.

When I glanced at Roddy again, he was leaning far back in his chair, his face slightly flushed. "S'okay," he was saying. "Anyhow, look. Seems like we got company."

Roddy was facing into the room, and I had my back to it. I twisted around, and, sure enough, Patty and

Mary Lou were threading their way toward us, their faces lit with expectant smiles.

They arrived at our table slightly breathless. "Ooh, Glenda, we saw you through the window," Mary Lou cooed. "I said to Patty, 'Now who's that with her?' "

Patty was already edging her way around the table with a slightly apologetic air. "I told Mary Lou it was probably Roddy, Glenda. Is this a private party? Or can we join you?"

I looked up and blinked. "It's not a party at all," I said, glancing at Roddy, whose face was expressionless. "Um, sit down, why don't you?"

Both girls sat down quickly, still smiling. Mary Lou looked from Roddy's place to mine. "You're both all finished?" She seemed disappointed.

"Yep, I'm done," Roddy said. He looked uncomfortable. I wondered if he was feeling embarrassed because of our conversation or annoyed because my two friends had just descended on us. He began to get up.

"Oh, why not stay a while," Mary Lou urged. "You seen any good horror movies lately? Where's, um, that friend of yours? Ethan."

Roddy shrugged. "Don't know." He turned to me. "Well, Glenda, guess I'd better be going. Happy birthday, again." He waved to the girls. "See ya around."

I looked after him, half wishing we hadn't been interrupted, even though we had gotten onto such an awkward subject and I'd started feeling guilty. We *could* have talked about something else. I never even found out what movies he'd checked out at the video store.

The moment Roddy was out of sight, Patty leaned forward eagerly. "What was *that* all about? Did we break in on something serious? You never told us you had a date with him, Glenda."

"Yeah," Mary Lou chimed in. "You're really a sly one. Did he take you out for your birthday or something?"

"He bought me a diet Coke," I said in a flat voice. "And it was no date. I just happened to run into him by accident."

Patty and Mary Lou looked a little let down.

"Well, um, don't be mad at us, Glenda," Mary Lou said softly. "We didn't mean to chase him away. If we did, that is."

"I'm not mad," I said grumpily. "I'm just . . . annoyed," I planted my elbows on the table and pushed away my empty cup, "at the way you two have been acting lately."

Patty gave me a hurt, wide-eyed stare. "You *are* mad. What did we do?"

"You sure know how to play Miss Innocent," I told Patty. "All week long, ever since Giselle got into our class, you two have been behaving like you hardly knew me. But today, all of a sudden, you see me with a boy and you come buzzing around like a couple of honeybees." I turned to Mary Lou. "*Where's that friend of yours, Ethan?*" I mimicked. "Do you actually think I can't see what's going on?"

Patty and Mary Lou exchanged glances.

"See, I'm right," I said.

Patty gave me a faint smile. "Well, Giselle's been following you around school all week like an elephant's shadow. Nobody could get near you if they tried."

"That's not funny," I snapped. "All those remarks about how big she is. Talking about her behind her back. Don't you think she knows? And even if she doesn't know, *I* know."

Patty was still smiling. "Honestly, Glenda, you're so serious lately. You just aren't any fun anymore."

"Oh, come off it," I said impatiently. "You two just don't want to know me when I'm with Giselle. Because she might be bad for *your* image. But it's altogether different when I'm with a boy. It's all a question of what's in it for you."

Mary Lou suddenly stood up indignantly. "Glenda, you are mean," she said. "Patty, I think we should go."

"Never mind," I said airily. "I'm leaving anyhow. I came downtown on my own today and that's how I'm going home."

I swept out of the fast-food restaurant without looking back. And, as for the video store, I didn't even glance toward it as I hurried by.

Chapter 8

"Glenda, hold still."

"How can I," I replied, "when you're pulling my head all to one side?"

"It's only until I get this gorgeous red-gold mop of yours under control," Giselle panted.

She'd been brushing and pulling, brushing and pulling my thick, crinkly hair for what felt like half an hour as I sat at the vanity table in my mother's bedroom. This was the Saturday evening that I thought I'd be spending alone in front of the TV. But it had turned out much better than I'd expected. Because Giselle had phoned me around suppertime, when she'd returned from the city, and we'd decided to get together at my house.

"What is it you're trying to *do* with my hair, anyway?" I asked Giselle. "You'll never get it straight and shiny. I've had wrinkled hair all my life."

Giselle's reply was muffled by the fact that she'd stuck a couple of hair clips between her pursed lips. "Just frying to poo it back."

I began to giggle but quickly winced as she took the clips out of her mouth and stabbed them into my scalp.

"Just trying to pull it back," she repeated, "to give you that clean-cut American girl look."

Staring into the mirror, I had to admit Giselle *was* creating a different me. The usual "Little Orphan Annie" frizz that encircled my face was gone. Giselle had cleared my forehead and swept my hair to one side. The new style made me look both younger and more sophisticated at the same time.

"Don't squirm now," Giselle cautioned as she lifted a can of hair spray with one hand and shaded my eyes with the other. The hair spray hissed and spritzed.

"This should hold it long enough to get you through an interview *and* a go-see," she said, setting the can down on the vanity table and backing away slightly to admire her work. Her hands flew into the air. "Voilà! The Wappington makeover."

I stood up and leaned closer to the vanity mirror. By restyling my hair and applying only a little makeup, Giselle had given me a new sense of myself. She'd patted on a complexion base about the same color as my freckles in order to conceal them slightly. She'd smeared vaseline on my bushy eyebrows and my eyelids. And she'd highlighted my lips and cheeks with pale pink gloss and blusher.

"So," I said, as I continued to admire myself in the mirror, "I'm all made up and no place to go. Why are we doing this? And what's a 'go-see,' anyway?"

"We're doing this," Giselle answered in her hearty voice, "because *next* week it's All-Girl or bust. And a 'go-see' is what the agency sends you on when you go see a client. Like maybe a wholesale manufacturer of plus-teen clothes who needs a showroom model," Giselle aimed her forefinger at me, "to show a new fashion line to buyers. You know, the folks who do the buying for specialty shops and department stores."

Mechanically, I began clearing and straightening my mother's vanity table. She had an eagle eye for anything that was ever out of place. "Great," I said. I was more impressed than ever with Giselle's abilities and knowledge when it came to modeling. "But what good's making plans? You know I can't go unless my mother comes along."

"Well, maybe we can think of a way to work that out," Giselle suggested.

"No way," I retorted, giving the vanity a final survey. "Listen, why don't we go inside and get ourselves a snack?" That was the trouble with food. It was such a comfort when there didn't seem to be an answer to something.

We headed for the kitchen, and Giselle sank into a chair while I rummaged through the refrigerator.

"So how was your day in the city?" I asked her as I started taking stuff off the shelves and out of the freezer compartment. Since Giselle didn't seem to be on a diet, I loaded up the table with whatever looked good. There was even some leftover birthday cake still in the freezer. I'd already experimented with eating it unthawed, and it was great. The frosting and filling tasted like ice cream.

Giselle sighed. "Oh, nice. I sort of poked around the

old neighborhood. Had a long chat with the doorman of our building."

I brought some glasses, plates, and forks to the table. "I guess you really miss your old friends, even though it's only been a couple of weeks since you moved. It must have been terrific to get together."

"Yeah," Giselle said, pouring herself a glass of diet soda (the only kind we had) and reaching for the birthday cake. "Except they were sort of scattered around this weekend. So I only saw one for a little while."

"That's probably my fault," I said. "If I'd known earlier in the week that I wouldn't be able to go in with you, you could have made plans with your friends."

Giselle cut a thick slice of chilled cake, added a generous scoop of ice cream, and daintily put a forkful in her mouth. "Oh, forget it. Like I said, we'll do it next week." Giselle looked up from her plate. "What did *you* do today?"

"Well," I mumbled, "I was kind of on my own. I bumped into Roddy Fenton, and we had a Coke together. He's this kid from school that I've known forever. Then Patty and Mary Lou came barging in and . . . and . . ."

I stopped, realizing that I couldn't tell Giselle what had actually taken place. Our argument had been all about her.

"And?" Giselle asked. I could detect the trace of a knowing smile playing around her lips. She was nobody's fool. The whole school was talking about her, and she knew it. It seemed a good time to try to change the subject.

"Nothing. At least nothing worth talking about," I said quickly. I took a gulp of soda and coughed a few times. "You know," I went on, "there's something I've been meaning to ask you, Giselle. How young *were* you when you got started in modeling?"

Giselle put an extra half scoop of ice cream on her plate. "Really young. About six months old. I did baby powder, diaper-rash ointment, and complexion-soap ads. My parents were both working for advertising agencies in those days. So, you know, it was easy to get their fat, cuddly little baby lots of exposure."

I tucked a few strictly forbidden potato chips into my mouth. They were from my hidden supply that I kept in a plastic garbage bag at the back of the broom closet.

"I see," I said slowly. This was getting interesting. Giselle hadn't told me about her parents before. "And then?" I prompted, nudging the potato chips in her direction.

"And then," she said, reaching out, "I got to be a toddler and started waddling around on my plump little legs. That's when I did the plush-toy ads and the building-block commercials."

"Hmm," I murmured. "I guess being a little fatty really paid off."

Giselle laughed her bubbly laugh. "Sure did. I was one baby who couldn't afford to lose her baby fat. So it just came along with me on a lifetime journey."

Lifetime journey . . . what a horrible thought! And to think it had all begun with Giselle's parents getting her those fat-baby jobs when she was too small to know what was happening. Then she had started growing up, still believing that fat was good. And by now, of course, her mountainous body was a mass of fat cells craving their daily calorie fix. From everything I'd read and heard on the subject, it was probably too late to do anything about it.

Instinctively, I pushed my chair back from the table, vowing not to let another morsel of snack food pass my lips. Because Giselle was my worst nightmare come true.

"You mean," I began hesitantly, "you, um, never tried to cut down a little?"

Giselle gave me an amused look. "Diet? What for? I could never lose enough to really matter."

I stared at her wordlessly. She had a point. And probably it hadn't mattered because she'd been doing fine at her old school with her old friends. So she'd just gone along being fat and happy.

I shrugged. "Well, I'm probably fighting a losing battle, too. It's just that I haven't got your . . . self-confidence. Every time I've been fat, people have started acting mean to me. And they made me feel . . . awful."

Giselle's smile had begun to fade. What was she really thinking, I wondered. Was she worrying that sooner or later she was going to lose touch with her friends in the city? Because it was going to be really hard to hold onto them from way out here in Havenhurst. Even today's visit to her old neighborhood sounded sad. She admitted that she'd spent most of the afternoon just talking to the doorman of the apartment building where she'd lived.

As for Giselle's future in Havenhurst, what did she have to look forward to? Immediately ahead lay another awful week at school. I wasn't the least bit sorry I'd told Patty and Mary Lou what I thought of them this afternoon. And scolded Roddy, too, for the way he'd laughed about the "blubber queen."

A few minutes later, Giselle said she thought she'd better be going. Walking the four or five blocks back to her house in the dark didn't hold any terrors for her after her years of getting around on her own in Manhattan.

"Now remember, Glenda, I'll be over here early next Saturday morning," Giselle said, fastening the ties on her oversize outer jacket, "to do your makeup and hair. And we'll talk at school during the week about what you should wear for the interview."

I gave her a questioning stare. "But wait a minute. We never even discussed what we're going to do about my mother. You told me yourself they don't like mothers of older kids coming along. And especially *my* mother. She'll talk their ears off and put on airs and make all sorts of demands. She'll spoil everything."

Giselle flurried her hands at me to try to quiet me. "Glenda, your mother isn't the one who's going to be applying for a modeling job. You are. If she insists on coming along . . . well, let her."

"Let her?"

"Yes, let her. Ever hear of the art of compromise?"

"Compromise?" I declared in exasperation. "That's just plain giving in."

Giselle shook her head. "Uh-uh. It's playing the game of trying to get what you want. Anyhow, what choice have you got?"

I gave Giselle a look of resignation. "None," I admitted.

Giselle patted my arm as I opened the door for her. "Good girl," she said approvingly. "Oh, and thanks for all the yummies."

"Thank *you* for the hairdo and stuff," I replied, patting my new stiffly sprayed coiffure and wondering what my mother would have to say about it.

As I watched Giselle make her way down the front walk and into the street, I offered up a silent prayer. All my life my mother had been trying to run the show for me. For once—just once—I prayed for some small miracle that would allow me to do things my own way.

Chapter 9

The following Saturday started out with everybody at my house having a case of the jitters. My mother had decided that driving to the station, parking the car, and taking the train into the city was a nuisance. She would simply drive all the way in with Giselle and me.

My father, who was up early for his golf game, was giving her all sorts of warnings and instructions as the three of us sat at breakfast. "You'll never find parking in that part of town, Grace. You'll have to go into a parking garage."

"I know that, Harold," my mother said, pouring her dry cereal into a bowl and munching on a few tidbits that had bounced into her lap.

"The weather looks iffy," my father remarked. "Take an umbrella with you. You'll never get into a garage that's really near the building you want."

My mother was trying hard to keep her cool. "I have an umbrella in the car, Harold."

"Be careful who gets into the elevator with you," my father cautioned. "Who knows what kind of building that modeling agency is in. Usually they're dumps."

"I can handle myself and the girls, Harold," my mother said smartly. "Why do you think I'm going along in the first place?"

"And call me," my father commanded. "Let me know what time you're leaving the city."

"How can I?" my mother asked. "You'll be out on the golf course."

"Not all day," my father said, finishing the last of his coffee and patting his moustache with his napkin. "Especially if it rains. Even if it doesn't, keep calling until you get me."

My mother rolled her eyes toward the ceiling as my father gave each of us a peck on the cheek and went out the side door to the garage. The next moment the front doorbell rang, and I went to let Giselle in.

"How nice you look, dear," my mother commented. Giselle was wearing a navy-blue jumper with a white turtleneck and a matching three-quarter-length navy jacket. "Do you think you'll be warm enough, though?"

"I'm never cold," Giselle said. She turned to me. "Well, should we start getting you ready?"

We hurried off to my room, where my clothes were neatly laid out and my makeup bag was nearly packed. Giselle and I had been adding useful items all week — cleansing cream in case I had to redo my makeup, cotton balls, a wide variety of cosmetics, a hairbrush, a teasing comb, hair spray, even a curling iron.

If I'd been an experienced model — which, of course, I wasn't — Giselle said I'd have had to bring along my portfolio with photos, tear sheets of magazine or newspaper ads I'd posed for, and so forth. But since I was a first-timer and didn't have any professional-type photos anyway, she said the best thing was just to go in and be "me."

"Now," Giselle declared, getting to work on my face and hair, "the magic word is *wholesome.* You're just a normal, natural, *slightly* plump, cheerful, healthy, clean-living, unassuming American girl. Got that?"

"Oh, sure," I said, trembling from head to foot as Giselle tried to lighten my flaming cheeks with the palest makeup base we had and started wrestling with my hair again. "I'm p-p-perfectly calm and t-t-t-totally at ease."

Giselle just grinned and ignored my tremors. "I'm doing your hair straight back this time, with a headband. It's a cleaner look, and you have such a good forehead. Also, it's the right hairdo for the Peter Pan collar with the little black bow-tie that you're wearing."

We had decided on a "classic" outfit consisting of a white cotton blouse and a dark tartan plaid skirt. Jeans or pants, Giselle said, were never a good idea for an interview, even if you were applying for a job as a skinny model. How in the world would I have known any of this if not for her?

By a quarter past eight, we were on our way out the door. My mother, of course, was dressed in one of her ladies' luncheon outfits, complete with brooch and matching earrings, and her ash-blonde hair was frozen into a mass of perfectly arranged ringlets and curlicues.

"Well, here we go," she said cheerfully as Giselle and I climbed into the back of the car and she settled herself in the driver's seat. "Off to conquer the big city."

Giselle glanced at me as if to say, "Courage!"

But I felt more like a sheep being led to slaughter than someone going off to conquer *anything*. I hadn't visualized our trip to Manhattan this way at all. I'd pictured Giselle and me taking the train together, feeling carefree and having fun as we set off on our little adventure. My mother's shepherding us had turned everything around for me.

At first the traffic was moderately light. But as we drove along, it began to thicken, growing more and more sluggish. I found myself peering into the cars alongside us. It seemed that everybody was headed for the tiny island between the rivers. And if even one in a hundred cars had a plump teenager with modeling ambitions in it, what a crush there'd be at the All-Girl Saturday-morning interviews!

I could hear my mother going "Tsk, tsk" in the front seat as we were forced to slow down to a series of jolting fits and starts. Of *course,* we should have taken the train. Even my father had voted in favor of it. But my mother had to have it *her* way.

I leaned over the front seat to look at the dashboard clock. Nearly an hour had gone by, and we were still miles from the nearest bridge or tunnel to Manhattan.

My only consoling thought was that maybe we'd miss the noon interview deadline entirely. And my disgusted mother would let Giselle and me try the train on our own the next week.

But finally, at around half-past ten, frazzled and jumpy, we were weaving our way through city streets toward the midtown address of the All-Girl agency. Even though she hadn't visited the place in years, Giselle guided my mother's car to the tall, nondescript office building with the instinct of a homing pigeon.

Of course, once we drove up to it, there weren't any curbside parking spaces. And any openings that did exist were ominously labeled TOWAWAY ZONE. That meant that a police tow truck could tow our car away to a pound at one of the distant edges of the city and hold it for ransom until my mother paid a whopping fine *plus* the towing charges. Naturally, this dire possibility had been included among my father's early-morning warnings.

"It's nearly eleven o'clock," I squeaked nervously after we'd attempted to go around the block a few times, getting caught by traffic lights and snarled in one-way streets that went the wrong way. Even the one or two parking garages we'd passed had signs out that said SORRY FULL.

Giselle leaned forward. "I know there's a big parking garage on Forty-fourth Street that always has room," she said. "It's only a few blocks from here. Maybe," she suggested to my mother, "you could drop us off near the building, so Glenda could get checked in before they stop seeing people. Then you could meet us up at All-Girl Models. The office is on the eleventh floor."

My mother looked around helplessly. We were standing at a traffic light that had just turned green, and the cars and trucks behind us had instantly set up a chorus of beeps. "Ah, um, well maybe that would be best," my mother murmured hesitantly.

I gave Giselle a grateful look. Just getting out of the car and walking to the building on my own would be a huge relief, assuming that I *could* walk without collapsing on the sidewalk into a bundle of quivering nerves.

"Now take care," my mother called out as she dropped us at the end of the block. "I'll just go up to Forty-fourth and park the car. And I'll see you soon."

"You're a genius," I declared to Giselle as the car sped away and I took a deep breath of damp autumn air laden with exhaust fumes. "I thought we'd keep on orbiting the neighborhood forever. My mother can be so stubborn. She probably wanted to be able to boast to my father that she found street parking."

Giselle just smiled and caught my hand. We dashed briskly toward the building entrance.

"Do they really stop letting people check in by a certain time?" I asked. To be honest, I was half hoping we might turn out to be too late. I was flushed and sweaty, and sure that I'd make a horrible impression on whoever was waiting to look me over.

"We're in time," Giselle said calmly as she shoved

me into a waiting elevator. It was dimly lit and fairly crowded. Instinctively, I turned around to see who else was in there. My father had said to be careful. He'd have had a fit if he'd known my mother wasn't with us.

Giselle nudged me hard, and I snapped my head around, eyes front.

"Don't you know about riding in elevators?" she remarked, after we'd picked our way out at the eleventh floor. "Don't act curious. Don't make eye contact. It can be embarrassing, and there are always strange characters around, besides."

"Sorry," I said, adjusting my clothes slightly and swallowing hard. I guess I'd acted like a country bumpkin. But I was *so* jittery.

We started down a long, echoing corridor with closed office doors on both sides. Then we made a sharp turn to the left. "Wait!" I panted, grabbing Giselle's arm. "Shouldn't we stop and look in a mirror or something. I must be a mess. I f-f-feel like a mess. I don't even know what I'm d-d-d-doing here."

Giselle paused, grabbed my shoulders, and turned me around slowly. "You're okay," she pronounced, lifting her right hand and making a circle with her thumb and forefinger. "Now keep your cool, Glenda. This is no time to go to pieces on me. And just remember . . . the key word is *wholesome.*"

With that, she yanked me through the doorway of the All-Girl modeling agency.

Chapter 10

I'm not sure what I expected to find on the other side of the clouded glass door announcing in fancy black lettering that this was the office of All-Girl Models. But, whatever it was, nothing had prepared me for the scene that greeted my eyes.

Suddenly, there we were, Giselle and I, in a chair-filled waiting room. It could have been a diet-doctor's office for overweight little girls of all ages. Their mamas sat beside them, some chatting to each other, others silent as if tensely waiting for a white-uniformed nurse to appear at any moment and call out, "Next."

A dark-haired, flawlessly made-up receptionist was seated at a desk just to the right of the entrance. "You here for the open call?" she inquired, looking up with a bored expression.

Giselle nodded toward me. "*She* is," she said.

The receptionist handed me a large white card. "Have a seat," she droned, "and fill this out."

Followed by curious and faintly hostile glances from some of the mothers and their chubby offspring, we made a beeline for a couple of empty chairs.

"I think we're in luck," Giselle whispered as we

settled ourselves. "I don't see anyone here your age. All these kids are younger. Not a one without a mama."

I breathed a temporary sigh of relief that my own mother hadn't escorted me through the door. It was bad enough that she'd be joining us after she parked the car. Maybe, somehow, the waiting room would have emptied out before that.

"What is this for?" I asked Giselle, holding up the white card the receptionist had given me.

"Just fill it out," Giselle said, "quickly." She dug a pen out of her purse, thrust it into my hand, and leaned over to help me with the blank spaces. Her fingertip flew from one box to the next. "Name, age, address, phone number, grade in school, height, weight . . ."

"My real weight?"

"Of course. You have nothing to be ashamed of. I told you it was perfect. Now keep going. Do all the vitals. Color of eyes. Color of hair. Dress size . . ."

I hesitated again. "Come on, come on," Giselle urged. "They don't expect you to be some ninety-pound miniskirter like Twiggy. This is the All-Girl agency, remember? There's *supposed* to be a lot of you. Well, a fair amount, anyway."

I wrote down my dress size and went on to chest, waist, and hip measurements, filling in the figures as closely as I could recall them.

"What about 'experience'?" I asked Giselle.

"None," she said, taking the card from my hands. "Believe me, they'll like your being simple, honest, and straightforward about yourself. Anyhow, there's no way you can fake it."

"And . . . and 'hobbies'?" I tried reaching for the card because it still had spaces on it I hadn't filled in.

But Giselle refused to give it back. "Forget the rest," she advised. "It's late, and I want to be sure you get interviewed today." With that, she rose and headed for the receptionist's desk with my application.

A few moments after Giselle had returned to her seat, the receptionist got up with a batch of white cards in her hand and disappeared through a door to an inner office.

"Now what?" I whispered to Giselle.

She looked around the room slowly. Nobody had been called since we'd entered the waiting room. There must have been eight or nine little kids squirming in their chairs and giving their equally impatient mothers soulful glances.

Giselle leaned closer to me. "Now just pray they happen to be looking for teenage models today so they pull your card out of the pile and call you in soon. Who knows, they might even send you on a go-see. Sometimes you can luck into a thing like that."

I shook my head. "This is too scary," I said, trying hard to take a deep breath. "It's like waiting to see the doctor. Or the school principal. And, besides, that outside door's going to open any minute, and my mother's going to walk in. I'll probably pass out."

Giselle poked her fleshy shoulder against mine.

"Oh, cheer up, Glenda. We got this far, anyway. Why don't you just think of it as an adventure, an adventure in which anything can happen —"

At that moment, the receptionist sauntered back into the room and everybody looked up alertly.

"Waite," she announced in a ho-hum voice.

Waiting, of course, was what all of us were doing. But Waite was also my second name. "Me?" I asked, aiming a finger at my pounding chest.

"Are you Glenda?" the receptionist demanded in a slightly impatient tone.

I nodded.

"Come on," she said. "Mrs. Mack'll see you now."

Giselle had already dragged me to my feet and was standing right behind me. "Go, go," she nudged me excitedly. "They want to take a look at you. This is great."

Trailed by Giselle, as well as a wave of resentful glances and fretful mutterings from the waiting room, I followed the receptionist into a narrow inner hallway. We passed a couple of doors leading off it. At the third door, a tall, imposing woman with gray-brown hair twisted into a stylish French knot stood waiting for us.

"Aha," she said, turning and signaling for Giselle and me to follow her into her office. "I'm Elayne Mack. Which one of you's Glenda Waite?"

I tried to speak, but only a hoarse crackling emerged from my lips. Mrs. Mack sat down at her desk and indicated the two chairs across from it. She glanced up from studying my application, which lay before her. "And you're . . .?" she questioned Giselle.

"Just a friend," Giselle said pleasantly, showing her usual self-confidence. "I recommended Glenda. I was an All-Girl model myself until, um, about six years ago."

"Really?" Mrs. Mack said with a certain aloofness. Maybe she didn't like the idea of a teenage applicant bringing a friend along. "The agency's changed hands, you know, since then," she remarked. "Still, we always appreciate good word of mouth."

I glanced hastily at Giselle. I'd been expecting a warmer reaction when she told them who she was. But Mrs. Mack didn't even ask her name, which didn't seem very kind after the way Giselle had paid for her fat childhood by becoming a teen who was too bloated to model anymore. Giselle, though, just sat there, her full, pink-lipped smile still turned on.

"So, Glenda," Mrs. Mack turned back to me. "You're fourteen. You'd like to do plus-size teen modeling. You have no experience. Is that your natural hair color?"

My hand flew to my head. "Oh, yes." The question had startled me. But this time my voice was clear.

"It's very pretty. Unusual, too. Do you wear glasses?"

"Um, no."

"Contacts?"

"No."

I must have looked puzzled by these questions—

ther had been ranting about and warning her against.

The picture of my mother sailing into Mrs. Mack's office grabbed me so hard, in fact, that I pushed my chair back abruptly, ready to get to my feet.

Mrs. Mack gave me a slightly puzzled look. "What is it, Glenda? I'm scaring you, aren't I? Well, that's part of my job. I'm not saying you couldn't do modeling work, mind you. But it does take something that you might not have, and that's toughness and determination."

Another put-down! Suddenly, the fire in my cheeks began to burn even more furiously, and words to match my indignation began rolling off my tongue like hot lava. "How do *you* know what I have and what I haven't got? How do *you* know what I can do and what I can't do?" I exclaimed. "You haven't given me a chance to *say* anything since I got here. All you've been doing is *telling* me what a big mistake it was for me to come here today!"

I got up and gave Giselle, who was still seated and looking at me in astonishment, a commanding look. "I'm sorry we took up your time," I said without even glancing at Mrs. Mack. "We've got to go now."

Mrs. Mack rose even before Giselle did. "Well," she remarked, "I see you *are* a feisty young woman. Maybe it's true what they say about redheads."

Her firmly composed features softened a little. "Let's not part on such an unpleasant note, though." To my surprise, her hand came reaching across the desk for mine.

Out of routine politeness, I gave it to her.

"Promise you'll think a little more about the things I've mentioned, Glenda," she said, still holding my hand. "Then you'll see I was only being fair and honest with you. I'm sorry I couldn't offer to register you with us now. But," she let go my hand and lifted the white card I'd filled in, "I'll hang onto this. For a while, anyway."

I led the way out to the waiting room with Giselle lumbering behind me and, sure enough, the first thing I saw was my mother arguing with the receptionist.

"Oh, thank goodness, my daughter *is* here," my mother shrilled, coming toward me with open arms the moment she caught sight of me. She looked flushed and distraught. "Glenda, darling, I only just got here. Can you believe it? Did I miss your interview entirely?"

I looked around us hastily and saw with relief that the waiting room was almost empty. The other applicants must have been called in to see some other interviewers. Or maybe they'd just gotten disgusted and gone home.

Giselle leaned toward my mother, who still had me tightly clasped in her embrace. "What happened, Mrs. Waite? Didn't you find the parking garage?"

My mother released me and dug into her purse for a lacy handkerchief to mop her brow with. "Garage?" she repeated. "The parking garage? Oh, I found that all right. It was *after* I parked the car that all the trouble began. I started to walk downtown a few blocks and then I realized I'd completely forgotten the address of the building. Do you know how many eleventh floors I rode up to in different buildings? Four, I think. Maybe five."

My mother went on refolding her hankie and dabbing at her forehead, chin, and throat. "But that's all unimportant now, darling," she said, turning to me. "Totally unimportant. Because I thought I'd lost you. And I found you at last." She lowered her voice to a confidential tone. "Just tell me, Glenda, how did the interview go? What happened in there?"

"Nothing happened," I replied in a perfectly normal voice, loud enough for the bored receptionist and the few people remaining in the waiting room to hear. "Nothing at all. In fact, we can all go home now."

Chapter 11

The next day, just as my parents and I were finishing a late Sunday-morning breakfast, the doorbell rang.

"That'll be Giselle for sure," I murmured as I got up from the table.

Things had been pretty low-key at my house since our return from the city the previous afternoon. By unspoken agreement, Giselle had remained silent on the drive home, letting me explain to my mother the reason for the failed interview at All-Girl Models. And I'd simply told her that they refused to register me because I lived too far from Manhattan.

I was careful, too — once we got home and I repeated the story to my father — not to mention anything about the up-front expenses for photos and stuff that Mrs. Mack had talked about, so there'd be no *I told you so's.* But, of course, my father did remind my mother that she'd "wasted" twelve dollars and fifty cents on parking fees as well as several gallons of gas.

My mother hadn't agreed it was a waste, though. "Nothing ventured, Harold, nothing gained," she'd told my father. "Glenda had a professional interview. It was an excellent learning experience for her." My mother didn't say anything, of course, about how she herself had gotten lost after parking the car and wandered around the neighborhood looking for the building in which the All-Girl agency was located.

As I approached the front door, I had to admit that my feelings toward Giselle since yesterday's visit to the city had become just a little wobbly. I'd been so sure she really knew "the modeling game," as she'd once put it. But yesterday in Mrs. Mack's office, even after I'd let go with my little tirade, Giselle had just sat there like a helpless has-been.

And since then, ugly little thoughts had started to creep around the edges of my mind. Had Giselle made more of her modeling experience and know-how because she wanted to win me over as a friend? Even worse, had *I* befriended Giselle because of what there might be in it for me — the chance to become a teen model?

Frowning slightly at my inward dilemma, I wrenched open the door. To my surprise, the looming figure of Giselle Wappington failed to materialize. Instead I looked down into the dark, mournful eyes of my friend — or maybe ex-friend — Patty.

The moment she saw my face, her right hand came up, palm out, in a gesture of self-defense. "Okay, okay, Glenda, slam the door in my face if you want to. You look so mad."

"Mad?" I mumbled, backing away. "No, I'm just surprised. I didn't expect . . ."

"I know, I know," Patty said, making no move to

come in. "But things are getting too unpleasant between you and me. We've known each other too long. I think we should talk."

"Well, okay," I said. The weather had turned much colder, and there was a cutting wind. Pretty soon, my parents would be calling out for me to close the front door because of the blast blowing through the house. "Come on in, why don't you? No sense standing out here and shivering."

Patty gave me a momentarily grateful glance and, rubbing her hands together, stepped carefully into our white-carpeted living room.

"It's Patty," I called to my parents out in the kitchen as we passed through the hall. "We're going to my room."

"That's fine, dear," my mother sang out after she and Patty had exchanged unseen hellos. I think my mother was actually glad to get rid of me. Suppose I accidentally blurted out to my father about her having gone off to look for the parking garage while Giselle and I rode the elevator to the eleventh floor of the All-Girl building unchaperoned?

"Oh, your room is so cozy," Patty murmured as she slowly unzipped her jacket. "That's new, isn't it?" She pointed to the boudoir chair my mother had gotten me as a welcome-home present when I'd returned from my summer job.

"You can sit in it if you want," I said matter-of-factly. "It's so dainty, it's more 'you' than 'me.' What's up, anyway?"

Patty made a big thing of snuggling into the flowered-chintz cushioning. "Your mother really has good taste," she sighed. "Why don't you sit down, too, Glenda? How can I talk to you if I'm sitting and you're standing?"

I dragged the chair out from behind my desk, turned it around to face her, and sat down.

"Glenda," Patty began, "you and I have to talk."

"You said that outside," I reminded her. "What about?"

Patty gave me a troubled look. "About whatever it is that's wrong between us since your birthday. Ever since . . . Giselle Wappington came on the scene."

I crossed my legs. "Fine," I said. "You started all this business of trashing Giselle. Maybe you'd like to explain it."

"Oh, Glenda," Patty protested, "that's an *awful* way to put it. You have to understand that she got me . . . upset . . . because, well, she was trying to take you over. You had been *my* friend for ages. And she seemed like such a know-it-all — smart kid from the big city, used to be a model, all that stuff. I figured she could make her own friends."

"Oh, sure," I said sarcastically, "at Havenhurst Junior High, where she's already been called all sorts of insulting names, and not without a little encouragement from the likes of you. Only last week I overheard 'Big Bird' and 'Pork Barrel.' If you were really my friend, you'd understand that making fun of her is just the same as making fun of me. Because I've lived through years of being 'Fat Glenda' at school and around this town."

"I know, I know," Patty declared, leaning forward earnestly. "I mean, I realize that I hurt *your* feelings by not being more sympathetic toward Giselle. Although she *is* three times your size, Glenda, at least. But actually that's what I came to apologize about."

"About hurting my feelings?"

"Yes. And Giselle's, too, of course. I think, um, that from now on we should all be friends. No more looking the other way when we bump into each other in class, no more sitting at separate tables in the cafeteria. Last week was really gross. Admit it."

"Sure it was," I agreed, recalling how unpleasant meeting up with Patty and Mary Lou in school had been after I'd told them off the Saturday before in the fast-food place. The only thing that had kept me going through the week was that I'd been looking forward to my secret visit to the modeling agency with Giselle. Only now, of course, my dream of getting to be a plump-teen fashion model had burst in my face like a big, gummy balloon.

"So we're friends again?" Patty inquired anxiously.

I sighed thoughtfully. It wouldn't be fair to Giselle if I said no. And why couldn't we all start doing things together now that nobody in the crowd seemed to feel it would be bad for her "image"?

"You're talking about Mary Lou, too, aren't you?" I remarked.

Patty slumped against the back of the chair. "Oh,

Mary Lou . . ." she moaned. "*That* one. Honestly, Glenda, she is such an airhead."

"Oh-oh," I said. "Something happened between you two." Instantly, my suspicions were aroused. Was this why Patty had come around to see me and started "making nice"?

"No, no," Patty said quickly. "Nothing happened between us. We didn't have a fight. It's just that she's been making such a fool of herself lately, you can't even talk to her."

"Fool?" I inquired. "How do you mean?"

Patty twirled a clump of her thick, dark hair. "Oh, you know, chasing boys. Running around after that friend of Roddy Fenton's."

I moved from the desk chair to the bed and made myself more comfortable. This was getting interesting. "Ethan," I said, with a knowing grin.

Patty nodded. "All week long she kept tracking him around school. A regular bloodhound. It was so embarrassing to be with her and watch her waggling her cute little fingers at him and making goo-goo eyes. Then she tried to get me to go to the video store with her on Friday afternoon because she found out he was going to be there, and I said no. For goodness sake, he's half a head shorter than she is."

"Well, so are most ninth-grade boys," I reminded Patty. "If you're tall like Mary Lou."

"Then she should find somebody in tenth grade. Or just forget the whole thing," Patty said coldly.

I stared at Patty. "Well, if Mary Lou doesn't mind

and Ethan doesn't either. . . . Did she find him over at the video store?"

Patty gave me a fierce look. "Yes, she did. And not only that. After he picked out his videos, she went over to *his* house with him and Roddy, and she *watched* a horror movie." Patty was speaking each word slowly and clearly for emphasis. "She was with *two* boys. And did she call me to invite me over? No!"

"Mary Lou watched a horror movie?" I exclaimed. "I can't believe it."

"Believe it, believe it," Patty said with mounting fury. "It just shows you how far she'll go to get a boy's attention. She told me herself that she screamed the whole time and gagged so much she was afraid she'd throw up. The boys must have thought she was going to flip out. Maybe they liked it. I don't know."

"So you *are* mad at her," I said softly.

Patty closed her eyes momentarily and shook her head back and forth. "No, I'm just disappointed. I always felt Mary Lou was immature. But now she's really proved it. After the video, she even got Ethan to walk her home because it was already dark out and she said she was scared to death."

I got up from my perch on the bed and went over to Patty "Maybe Mary Lou is immature," I agreed, "but she seems to be having better luck with boys than most of us. Goodness knows, I don't have a boyfriend and I guess you don't either. So why don't we just forget the whole thing and go inside and get ourselves a snack or something?"

Patty jumped up from the chair and put her arm around my waist. "Glenda," she murmured blissfully, "you are *such* a good friend. I just knew you'd understand."

I understood all right as, arms entwined, Patty and I awkwardly bumped our way through the hall that led to the kitchen. I understood that Patty was envious of Mary Lou's success with Ethan, that my own summer romance with Justin was as dead as the swirling autumn leaves, and that somehow the sad souls of this world — like Patty, Giselle, and me — would probably always end up sticking together.

Chapter 12

"Can I ask you something, Glenda?"

Almost a week had gone by, and Giselle and I were in the girls' room between fifth and sixth period, staring into the mirror and primping in an idle sort of way. I'd gone back to my old hairdo, a curly frizz encircling my face. There didn't seem to be much point in striving for a new look now that I was the old me again. And, true to form, I'd gained another pound and a quarter since my visit to All-Girl Models. Why not? It was the natural result of being frustrated and disappointed.

"Sure, what is it?" I mumbled as I tried to untangle some knotted tendrils of hair over my right ear.

Giselle spoke directly to my image in the mirror. "I've been asking myself this question for days," she said in an unusually sober voice. "So now I'm going to ask *you*. Are you just a teeny, teeny bit angry with me?" Giselle put her head to one side and held up her thumb and forefinger, holding them close together but not touching.

I felt a stab of discomfort. Because I thought I'd been doing a pretty good job of concealing my thoughts about how maybe Giselle and I were just using each other instead of really being friends.

"No, I'm not angry," I said quickly, turning from the mirror and facing Giselle. "Why should I be?"

Giselle finished running a comb through her thick, close-cropped hair. "Well," she said, tucking the comb into the huge shoulder purse she always carried, "you've been acting pretty cool about what happened last Saturday, which is fine because it shows you really are a strong person, Glenda. But I also can't help thinking that you're kind of annoyed with *me*. Maybe you think I let you down. Do you?"

Just then the warning bell rang for sixth period, and I scrambled to get my things together. "It wasn't your fault," I said, busily rearranging my books. "I guess you just didn't know enough about teen modeling. Or how hard it would be to get a job in the city from way out here in Havenhurst. After all, it wasn't part of your experience."

Giselle still looked doubtful. But before either of us could say anything more, we found ourselves pushing our way out into the crowded school corridor and streaming toward our next class. As usual, Giselle was getting a number of goofy stares and sly grins from the kids coming toward us. You'd have thought that by this time everyone in Havenhurst Junior High would have adjusted to her dimensions and quieted down a bit. But, no, there always had to be a few clowns.

It was actually a relief to get to the doorway of our English classroom, where Patty was waiting for us with a sour expression on her face. I couldn't tell whether she was looking glum because Giselle and I had stopped in the girls' room together or because, just across the hallway, Mary Lou and Ethan were standing in a recessed area and holding a private conversation.

To tell the truth, I was getting tired of everybody being so picky and suspicious these days. Giselle was probably wondering why Patty was being friendly to us again and worrying that I might be thinking of dumping *her*. Patty was watching Mary Lou's every move and seething at the way she'd managed to get one of the best-looking boys in ninth grade to follow her from one class to another. And *I* was trying to keep peace with all three girls, while still brooding over my own hurt feelings and the way nothing ever seemed to break right for me.

"What's with *you*?" I asked Patty as we drew closer to her.

Patty jerked her chin in Mary Lou's and Ethan's direction. "The lovebirds are at it again," she murmured. "He's met her at every single period break since she left homeroom this morning. I don't see how he ever gets to any of his own classes on time."

Giselle chuckled. "On wings of love," she suggested.

But Patty didn't think that was funny. "You'd imagine he'd get a stiff neck having to hold his head back so he can look up into those watery blue eyes of hers," she hissed.

"Some men may actually like to have their women

taller than they are," I remarked. "Who says it always has to be the other way around?" But, of course, I knew what was troubling Patty. Ethan was exactly the right height for *her.* Yet he'd hardly ever noticed her when she was with Mary Lou.

"Let's face it, girls," Giselle said consolingly. "Blondes are supposed to have more fun. Maybe they do."

"Sshhh!" Patty commanded suddenly. "They're breaking up. Here she comes. Let's go get three seats together. I don't care what Mr. Mintz says about assigned seats. I won't sit next to her."

Mary Lou came into the room with a sheepish smile on her face that quickly turned to puzzlement when she noticed that Patty had changed her seat. In a way, I couldn't help feeling sorry for Mary Lou as she gingerly went to her usual place, realizing that she'd been deserted. Maybe she wouldn't have had to pay such an awful price for her newfound romance if at least she'd invited Patty to join her for the horror-movie video at Ethan's house last Friday. Still . . .

Mr. Mintz rapped his desk for attention, and I tried my best to settle down and concentrate on the Shakespeare play we were studying. But it was hard to resist turning around to peek at Mary Lou, who was sitting behind us and slightly to our left. *Ah, love,* I thought. Mary Lou's expression was dreamy. For the time being, anyway, she didn't seem to be suffering too much from Patty's resentment of her romance with Ethan. It was easy to be wrapped up snugly in a world of your own when there was a very special boy in your life. I knew this from my summer's experience with Justin, and somehow from deep inside me an involuntary sigh — or maybe it was a groan — welled up and escaped from my throat.

The sound I made must have been noisier than I thought, because Mr. Mintz actually turned from the blackboard and both Patty and Giselle poked me hard. Then, oddly, a split second later, the loudspeaker system over Mr. Mintz's head opened up with its angry crackling that regularly preceded some message from the main office. Mr. Mintz stopped talking while we all prepared to listen to an overbearing voice making announcements that never seemed to have anything to do with the classroom that was getting them — an after-school club meeting, a new time for basketball practice, a changed bus schedule.

I was in the middle of a yawn, waiting with all the others, when a sharp woman's voice on the speaker exploded into the English classroom. "GLENDA WAITE, GLENDA WAITE TO THE MAIN OFFICE." There was a second's pause while I sprang to attention, my heart thumping. Then the message was repeated. "GLENDA WAITE TO THE MAIN OFFICE. IMMEDIATELY."

The loudspeaker shut off, and Mr. Mintz waved an impatient hand of dismissal at me. I had already tucked my purse under one arm and was reaching for my books with the other. "Should I take everything?" I whispered frantically to Patty and Giselle. "What could it be? I never was called . . ."

"Yes," Giselle hissed back. "Take all your stuff. You never know." She and Patty looked up at me with concern as I shuffled out into the aisle and made for the door of the classroom. The back of my neck and my ears were burning. I hated being singled out, especially when I was looking as fat as I was these days. And why was I being commanded to appear in the main office?

Kids who'd gotten into serious trouble got called to the office. Kids who had some emergency at home got called to the office. . . . Half running, puffing hard, I rushed along the empty second-floor corridor to the staircase and stumbled down it to the main floor of the school building. Here a few more people could be seen, kids on errands, one of the school custodians, two teachers talking in soft voices.

I raced past them, targeting my leaden body for the main office like an unwilling cannonball. At the glass-paned door, I paused for just a moment. Nothing unusual seemed to be going on inside. The clerks sat at their desks behind the long wooden counter. Beyond them lay various inner doorways, one of them leading to the principal's office. Who was I supposed to ask to see, anyway?

Panting, I turned the doorknob, staggered inside, and dumped my books and purse on the wooden counter. "I'm here," I gasped to nobody in particular. "Glenda Waite."

One of the clerks looked up absently from her typing. "Glenda who?"

I repeated my full name. "They sent for me. On the loudspeaker. In Mr. Mintz's English class. On the second floor."

The clerk got up slowly. "Just a minute," she said. "I'll try to find out what this is all about."

I leaned my elbows on the counter and rested my chin between my hands. The tom-tom in my chest was thumping louder than ever. My palms came away from the sides of my face moist with perspiration. What could I have done? Cut a class? Failed to hand in a homework assignment? Talked in study hall? Nobody, but nobody, got called to the office for puny little offenses like those. Not these days.

I cast my eyes down in worried despair. What was taking so long? Had the whole thing been a mistake? It was only twenty minutes past two, and my English class had more than half an hour to go. I'd feel so stupid slinking back into Mr. Mintz's room, everybody staring at me. . . .

"Glenda! Darling." I looked up in shock as an all-too-familiar voice hurled itself at me. Sure enough, there was my mother emerging from one of the doorways behind the clerks' desks and waving a slip of yellow paper at me. She hastily came around to my side of the counter, breathing hard. "I'm *so* glad to see you, darling. What *took* you so long?"

"What is it?" I gasped in a panicky voice. "Is anything wrong?"

My mother grabbed my arm to point me toward the office door, while I reached around awkwardly for my books and purse, still resting on the counter. "I'll tell you outside," she breathed in my ear. "This is our exit pass." She fluttered the yellow paper before my eyes. "We have to hurry."

"Why, why?" I demanded as she propelled me along the main hallway to the street door. For the second time in a month, I felt like I was being kidnapped by my own mother.

"The car's right outside," my mother said urgently. "I'm not even sure I parked legally. There just wasn't time."

She was already opening one of the heavy wooden doors to the outside of the school building.

I shrank back as a puff of cold air hit me. "My jacket," I said. "I haven't got my jacket. It's in my locker."

"Oh, no," my mother moaned. "Silly, silly me. I nearly forgot. Imagine if you went out without a coat in this weather and caught your death. At a time like this." She thrust the yellow exit pass into my hand and grabbed my armful of books. "Go get it this minute, darling. And meet me in the car. I'll have the motor running."

I gave her a harried glance and dashed down the corridor to my locker. Fortunately, it was on the main floor. A few moments later, I had one arm in my jacket sleeve and was bounding down the school steps toward the waiting car. As soon as I was inside and had slammed the door shut, my mother gunned the engine and we shot forward like a pair of bank robbers in a getaway car.

I turned to my mother. "We're alone now," I said exasperatedly. "We're out of the school building. Do you mind telling me what this is all about?"

My mother's fierce behind-the-wheel expression softened and gradually became a broad, self-satisfied smile. "It's *only* your big chance, sweetheart," she announced triumphantly. "A real offer of a modeling job. Oh, I can't wait to see your father's face when I tell him."

"A modeling job?" I gasped. What on earth was my mother talking about?

"Yes," she went on complacently. "And how lucky it was that I was home this afternoon when that phone call came. Because we have to be there by three o'clock. And I don't intend for us to be late."

I looked at the clock on the dashboard. It was a little past two-thirty. "Be *there*? Where? What *kind* of a modeling job? How did it happen?" I could feel my breath being choked off because my heart seemed to have leapt right into my throat. But the more excited I became, the calmer my mother got.

"Relax, Glenda, dear," she said in her maddening way. "And I'll tell you all about it."

Chapter 13

With a sharp squealing of brakes, my mother steered the car into the main entrance of the Havenhurst Shopping Mall. It was nearly ten minutes to three on the dashboard clock.

"So you see why I had to come to school and get you dismissed early, Glenda," my mother explained as she efficiently wove her way through the traffic lanes that skirted the parking areas. "I told the assistant principal it was for an important after-school job interview. Which it is. So you can't say I was lying."

I was still shaking my head in amazement at what my mother had reported to me on our drive to the mall. And now that we were there, we were heading straight for Ballard's, the biggest and most expensive of the mall's three department stores.

"But I . . . I didn't think Mrs. Mack liked me at all," I stammered in my continuing confusion. "In fact, I . . . well, I kind of yelled at her on Saturday because she seemed to be putting me down the whole time and she wouldn't let me talk."

Even though my mother's story had been simple enough on the surface, the pieces hadn't quite fallen into place for me yet.

It seemed that around two that afternoon the All-Girl modeling agency had called my house asking to leave a message for Glenda Waite. My mother said she'd take the message, and then this woman had come on the line and announced that she was Mrs. Mack, who'd interviewed me on Saturday.

My mother, of course, had gotten all excited. But Mrs. Mack had firmly stated that the agency still couldn't offer to register me. The only reason she was calling was that she'd just learned that the Ballard's branch store out in Havenhurst was planning a teen-clothing promotion this month. And she'd remembered that I lived in Havenhurst. If I wanted to try for a spot in the promotion on my own, I could apply directly to the store's fashion coordinator. End of message.

Never one to let the grass grow under her feet, my mother had phoned the store and learned they were interviewing both regular and plus-size teens today and tomorrow only. She'd promptly made an appointment for three o'clock, figuring that was the best way to beat the after-school crowd.

"And here we are," my mother announced buoyantly as she shot into a freshly vacated parking space near the front entrance of Ballard's.

"Yes," I repeated as I lurched backward in my seat. "Here we are. Only what do I look like? My hair, my clothes, my makeup. Everything's terrible. I feel all grungy from school. It's all too . . . sudden."

“Nonsense,” my mother replied. “We’ll just have to make the best of things. If we hurry, we’ll have time to stop in the ladies’ lounge and freshen you up a bit. How many plump teens with your pretty face and hair do you think are going to show up, anyway?”

It was nice that my mother was so confident. But I couldn’t help wishing, as we passed through the perfumed entrance into the subdued elegance of Ballard’s, that Giselle was here with me instead. If there ever was a case of a typical “stage mother” dragging her kid in for a job interview, this was it. And this time, unlike my visit to the All-Girl agency, there would be no getting away from my mother’s overbearing and sure-to-be embarrassing presence.

About five minutes later, fresh from a face wash and a hair combing in the ladies’ room, we were on the second floor of Ballard’s asking our way to the fashion coordinator’s office. Everything about the store felt a little intimidating — the too-thick taupe-colored carpet, the soft lighting and background music, the sophisticated-looking clothing on the racks, even the salespeople, most of whom looked like high-fashion models themselves.

Even my gung ho mother actually knocked a little timidly, I thought, on the burnished mahogany door marked PRIVATE, where we were supposed to see a Miss Oliver. A moment later the door was opened by a stunningly dressed woman with theatrical features and a striking blonde pageboy hairdo.

"Y-e-e-e-s?" she inquired.

My mother told her who we were and who we were looking for.

"That's me," the woman replied in a vaguely foreign accent. "Come in, da-r-r-lings. Let me see what we have here." I couldn't make out whether her accent was French, Hungarian, German, or Russian, or a peculiar mixture of all of them.

We were in a large room that was part office, part fitting room, part workroom. At one end there were groups of half-clothed department-store dummies, some cutting tables, and a pair of sewing machines. But no one else was in the room, which was a relief to me. I'd had visions of another waiting room like the one at All-Girl Models. Only this time the fat kids would all be teenagers like me.

"So you're the one for the plus-size fashions. Take off your jacket please, da-r-r-ling. Don't be shy. I was plump, *much* fatter than you, once. Now see, I'm svelte. It makes no matter."

Miss Oliver pirouetted to show us her lovely figure, while my mother, mumbling words of admiration, helped me remove my jacket and began to fuss with my hair and clothes.

Suddenly, Miss Oliver lifted her shoulders and pointed an imperious finger at my mother. "Now, Mama," she ordered, "go sit down and let your daughter walk a little bit for me. You ever been on a runway, da-r-r-ling?"

"No," I replied, remembering Giselle's advice and giving her a straightforward answer. "The truth is I have no modeling experience at all. But I do think I have the right plus-teen measurements. Um, I can write them all down for you."

Miss Oliver raised her arm with a jangling of golden bracelets. "No need. Measurements I can see with my eyes. Experience, too, I don't care about. If you can learn, we teach you. It's really simple. Now, just walk from one end to the other, thinking always in your mind like this." Miss Oliver pointed her forefinger in the air. "You are in a crowded room. You are wearing beautiful clothes. You are walking on a raised platform about three feet high. It's narrow, so don't go dizzy. Walk to the end. Graceful. Not too slow. Turn. Come back. Turn again to show the clothes. Walk some more. . . ."

As Miss Oliver went on to re-create the typical fashion-show scene, one that I remembered all too well from my birthday lunch in the banquet room of the Holiday Park Motel, I tried to put myself in the place of the models I'd watched. Maybe it was Miss Oliver's intriguing accent, which seemed to lightly fade in and out, or the dramatic lilt of her voice. Anyway, she managed to put me in the right mood. I could almost see myself on that glittering runway as I sashayed smoothly from one end of the room to the other, obeying her commands.

"Good!" she pronounced. I dared to look at my

mother for the first time. She had been cowering quietly in a pink-upholstered, gilt-trimmed chair ever since Miss Oliver had ordered her to go and sit down. Now she was rising to her feet, all smiles. But Miss Oliver was too quick for her.

"Sit, sit, my dear lady. I don't make your daughter a runway model so fast."

Slightly deflated, my mother sank down into her chair while Miss Oliver came over to me and grasped my shoulders with her surprisingly strong beringed fingers. "I tell you what, though, Miss Glenda. I give you a chance. The big fashion show is not till later in month, so we will see. But for now, I can give you some informal floor modeling. You know what this is?"

I shook my head. "No. I'm . . . not sure I do."

"Okay. I tell you. Today is Thursday. You come in on Saturday morning. Early. We fit you with three, maybe four outfits from the new plus-teen line. About eleven o'clock you go on the floor dressed in first outfit. Just yourself. You walk around in junior department and also on main floor, which is most crowded. You have small card to show, announcing what you wear and department that clothes are from. You smile, walk, just informal. Change outfits. Repeat. Until four, maybe five o'clock."

Miss Oliver nodded, her artfully made-up eyes searching my face.

"Just me?" I asked. "I mean, will there be other models walking around, too?"

"Almost for sure," she replied. "But plus-size teens,

I don't think. This is something new." Miss Oliver looked up and addressed my mother with a wry smile. "In this country, over thirty million ladies and young girls are too fat. But fashion models are skinny. Makes no sense."

Encouraged by Miss Oliver's remarks, my mother got up and rushed over to where we were standing. "You're so right," she gasped. "I couldn't agree more. It's about time some attention was paid to us heavier gals. Will, ah, Glenda be paid for modeling on Saturday?"

Miss Oliver's eyes widened. "Of course. Good hourly rate, from time she comes in for fitting." She turned to me. "You bring your own shoes, da-r-r-ling. I tell you what kind. Also what you must bring for hair, makeup, and so forth. Now we all go to desk to look over agreement form and Mama will give her signature."

As we followed Miss Oliver's fashionably slender figure to the paper-strewn desk, my mother squeezed my arm so tightly that I let out a short, involuntary shriek of pain. Miss Oliver turned to look at me in momentary alarm. But all she said was, "You have Social Security number, da-r-r-ling? If not, you get one quick, yes?"

Chapter 14

There was no getting off the phone with Giselle when I got back from my fashion-modeling interview at Ballard's. So, at my mother's suggestion, I invited her to have dinner with us that evening.

As a celebration, my mother took a pile of thick steaks out of the freezer and got to work making her famous home-fried potatoes and double-creamed spinach, all great big no-nos as everyday fare at our dinner table.

"But *this* is a special occasion," my mother announced as she took her seat at the table and began passing the generous, steaming platters around.

Giselle, her shiny cheeks flushed a deeper shade of pink than usual, helped herself with a smile of appreciation. "Everything looks delicious, Mrs. Waite." She beamed as she tucked into her food.

My father sat at the head of the table, cutting his porterhouse steak into neat, geometric pieces. "*You're* very quiet this evening, Harold," my mother remarked. "Aren't you just bursting with pride at your daughter's getting a fashion-modeling job on only her second try?"

My father nodded. "Of course, of course. But let's not count our chickens, Grace. So far it's only one day's work Glenda's been promised. Let's see if she even likes it."

I exchanged glances with Giselle. Naturally, my father was going to take a "wait-and-see" approach. He couldn't afford to admit to my mother that she'd been right to be so optimistic about my future as a plump-teen model. And, secretly, I too wondered whether I would like strolling around Ballard's as an oversize store mannequin come to life.

Who knew what sort of outfits they would dress me in? I hadn't seen any of the clothes yet. Suppose they were really weird. I was basically shy and self-conscious. How was I going to feel, smiling at strangers who were *supposed* to stare at me, maybe even ask me questions or want to examine the clothes I was wearing?

My mother looked up from buttering a hot roll. "Oh, she'll love it, Harold," she assured my father. "And I *know* Glenda will be in the big runway show later in the month. I could see that the fashion coordinator at Ballard's really liked her." My mother passed the rolls and butter to me. "Didn't she, dear?"

I nodded "yes" to Miss Oliver's appearing to like me and shook my head "no" to the rolls and butter. A peculiar knot had been forming in the pit of my stomach ever since we had sat down to our festive meal.

"Of course, it's Giselle we really have to thank," my mother went on, offering around the deep-fried onion rings she'd decided to add to the dinner menu at the last minute. "If not for Giselle's idea about going into the city for that interview at All-Girl Models last week, none of this would be happening. And you," she added pointedly for my father's benefit, "were *so* against it, Harold."

Giselle smiled sweetly and took a second helping of onion rings, while my father went on eating as though he hadn't even heard his name mentioned. My mother just shook her head with a triumphant smile and passed the onion rings to me. But I politely declined.

"Not hungry, Glenda?" she inquired. "You can indulge yourself a little. How much could you possibly gain between now and Saturday? Remember what Miss Oliver said. Skinny models are a dime a dozen. It's the plump ones that are finally in demand."

"I know," I murmured. But the vision I had of a scared-to-death me floor modeling among the Saturday crowds at Ballard's just wouldn't go away. And the knot in my stomach kept on twisting and swelling like a great coiling snake.

"You'll have to tell the other kids at school, Glenda," Giselle remarked matter-of-factly as my mother brought out the freezer dessert she'd concocted, which she called mud pie. It was a layered mixture of chocolate brownies and vanilla ice cream, topped with hot fudge sauce. "Well, Patty, anyway," Giselle went on. "And what will you do about Mary Lou?"

"Oh, I never even thought about that," I exclaimed, staring down at the too-big portion of gently oozing and melting mud pie my mother had just set before me. "Do I *have* to tell them?"

But even as I spoke, I realized that Patty would want to know why I'd been called to the main office during English class that afternoon, and so would Mary Lou. And I'd have to explain, too, about Giselle's attempt to get me into teen modeling through the All-Girl agency — which seemed to have failed at first and then led to my job at Ballard's after all.

Patty, especially, would be furious that she hadn't known about any of this before. She'd even resented Giselle's having once been a model. Yet how angry could Patty afford to get now that she'd broken off her friendship with Mary Lou?

"Do you think," I said, taking a small spoonful of my dessert and pushing the rest away, "that my friends from school might actually come to see me modeling at Ballard's on Saturday?"

"Well, you know *I'll* be there for sure," Giselle replied. "And why not the others? The more the merrier. The reason you're modeling, Glenda, is to attract people into the store and get them to buy things."

I planted my elbow on the table and dropped my chin into the palm of my hand. "It's all getting so . . . complicated," I sighed worriedly.

My father put down his coffee cup. "You see, Grace," he said. "It's going to be too much for Glenda. I was afraid of something like this."

"Nonsense," my mother exclaimed airily. "If you're concerned about Glenda's not eating, Harold, it's because she's just a little overexcited. Who wouldn't be? I'll see that she has something later on."

But, nevertheless, my mother got up and came around the table to feel my forehead and the back of my neck. "When Giselle finishes her dessert," she suggested soothingly, "why don't the two of you go off to your room, Glenda, and just relax. Giselle can help you get to work on that list of pantyhose and makeup and things that Miss Oliver told you to bring with you on Saturday."

I nodded in agreement, and a few minutes later Giselle and I left the table together.

"I don't get it," I whispered to Giselle as we started down the hallway toward my bedroom. "I always eat even more than usual when I get nervous or stressed out about something. But all of a sudden, there's this . . . change. I finally get a job as a fat-teen model. And the first thing that happens to me is that I completely lose my appetite."

"So da-r-r-ling, turn one more time."

It was around eleven o'clock on Saturday morning and, at last, I was ready to leave the fitting room. For the past couple of hours, I'd been twisted and twirled, patted and pulled at by a pair of "sewing ladies" with pins in their mouths, all under the critical eye of Miss Oliver.

"This outfit is ado-r-r-able," Miss Oliver pronounced with satisfaction. "It's like a baby Chanel—

that sweet jacket with the gold buttons, that short skirt with just a little flare, even the pocketbook."

I took a last look at myself in the mirror. I'd been learning fast that Chanel was the name of a woman who'd been one of the great fashion designers of all time and whose "classic" styles were still popular. The short, tailored, pumpkin-colored jacket I'd been buttoned into was okay. But I thought the charcoal-gray skirt that went with it was too short for my well-rounded knees and thighs. Miss Oliver assured me, though, that the "look" was exactly right with the dark pantyhose I was wearing.

The thing that *really* got to me was the little matching, derbylike hat with the rolled brim that Miss Oliver had jammed onto the top of my head. It just sat there, absolutely straight across the tops of my eyebrows, like an overturned pot. Aside from thinking I looked really dumb, I couldn't help wondering what teenager — skinny *or* fat — would ever wear a hat like that.

I reached up to touch the hard, rounded, felt surface of the hat.

"Ah-ah, da-r-r-ling. Don't touch," Miss Oliver cautioned. "All is now perfect. We put you down directly on the main floor."

I gave her a look of dismay. "Not in the junior department first?" That was what Miss Oliver had more or less promised on Thursday. And I knew I'd feel safer tucked away on the second floor while I sort of "tried on" my job of parading around the store holding the announcement card that explained about the outfit I was modeling.

But Miss Oliver responded by shaking her head and taking a surprisingly firm hold of my left elbow. "No, no, da-r-r-ling. We do not waste such a good new line. We do a *big* promotion. Come, I take you downstairs on the floor myself."

I must have been holding back because I could feel Miss Oliver tugging at me while my feet remained glued to the ground. The two sewing and fitting ladies stood side by side, their hands folded in front of them, watching. I couldn't tell what they were thinking.

Suddenly, Miss Oliver let go of me. Her eyes became enormous orbs, and her generous, lipsticked mouth curved into an almost terrifying smile. "What? You don't go? We work so hard to make you beautiful model and you show yourself to be a baby? What will your mama say, da-r-r-ling?"

The mention of my mother, who had dropped me off before the store even opened and then been banished until eleven o'clock by Miss Oliver, was all it took to jolt me out of my paralysis. Stage fright or no, I knew I had no choice now but to meet my "public."

And, sure enough, the moment Miss Oliver gently pushed me through the door marked PRIVATE, there were my mother and Giselle, huddled just outside it.

"Fantastic!" Giselle hissed, while my mother made some sort of sound halfway between a swoon and a war whoop. Then, without another word, the two of them fell into step behind Miss Oliver and me, as I was grimly marched to the top of the down escalator.

As we paused for just a moment, I looked in terror at the sea of heads just below me. I knew my cheeks were fiery beneath the makeup that Miss Oliver herself had carefully applied. At the same time, my hands were icy and my knees felt like Jell-O. Already the people we'd passed on the second floor had turned to look at me.

It was that hat more than anything else, I was sure — that hat and the stagy makeup I was wearing and my carroty hair, and the little fitted jacket with all the brassy gold buttons on it.

And, as we boarded the escalator and started to roll downward, it struck me that I knew *exactly* what I looked like. An organ-grinder's monkey. All I needed to complete the picture of myself that was bouncing around in my head was a long tail and a little tin cup!

Chapter 15

For the next ten minutes, I followed Miss Oliver around in a terrified daze as she showed me where to walk and where to pause in making my rounds on the main floor of Ballard's. Nor did it help any that my mother and Giselle kept trailing us. Even worse, they managed to creep up to me every now and then with approving comments about how stunning I looked and how much attention I was getting from the passing shoppers.

"Mama and girlfriend," Miss Oliver finally ordered, as she herself made ready to leave me, "it is best now that you should go. Our little girl must work."

With relief, I watched my mother and Giselle as they reluctantly left the store to do some errands elsewhere in the mall. And, soon after, Miss Oliver, too, vanished, promising to send for me when it was time to change into the next outfit I was to model.

At last I was on my own, a plump-teen floor model in an eye-catching getup that was sure to attract curiosity and comment. But, after all, that was my job. And, strangely enough, once I'd made a few rounds, I discovered that I felt less self-conscious and uncomfortable among strangers than I had with the people who knew me. Maybe being a fashion model was sort of like having the lead in the school play. The performance that made you the most jittery was the one with all your relatives and friends sitting out front, wearing expectant grins on their faces.

"Such a smart little outfit," one elderly blue-haired shopper remarked to her friend as she fingered the sleeve of my jacket. "Maybe the days when young girls dressed like ladies will come back after all."

I smiled sweetly and reminded her, as Miss Oliver had instructed me, of the plus sizes that my outfit came in.

"Very suitable," the woman's companion said. "If there's anything I hate to see it's a fat girl in jeans."

Wincing, I passed on along my route. I myself had always been a "fat girl in jeans" and still was — at least whenever I could find a pair roomy enough to zip up.

Other people didn't talk to me about my clothes at all. They assumed I was some sort of walking information center and wanted to know where the sleepwear department was, where they could find the reversible bath mats that were on sale, or whether there was a drinking fountain on the main floor.

"Hmmm?" a fortyish woman with a frowning expression said as she stood in front of me, talking more to herself than to me. "I didn't know hats were coming back. Maybe they are. But then again maybe they aren't." Then she simply walked away.

But even that, or the people who stared open-mouthed when I came into view and stood looking speechlessly after me as I passed, didn't upset me too much. Because I don't think any of them thought of me as a real person. So, in a way, neither did I. I was just this moving body, displaying an outfit that had been dreamed up on some designer's drawing board. And, thinking about my work as a floor model that way, I actually began to relax a little.

As noontime approached, Ballard's main floor seemed to get even more crowded than before. I was actually having a little trouble squeezing through the aisles and was just rounding the semiprecious jewelry counter when I heard an ear-piercing shriek.

"Ooh, it's true. There she is!"

The next moment Mary Lou Blenheim was racing toward me, her eyes wide and her pale hair flying. Before I could stop her, she'd thrown her arms around me, knocking my rolled-brimmed hat slightly to one side.

"Ooh, ooh, sorry," she gasped, backing away and raising her hands to straighten it. "I just got *so* excited seein' you, Glenda. You look . . . fabulous. Is it true they're actually payin' you and all? Do you get to keep any of these clothes? I mean you're a real model, aren't you?"

"Sshhh. Not so loud, Mary Lou," I cautioned, turning to quickly check my hat, hair, and makeup in the mirror on the jewelry counter. "No, I don't get to keep the clothes. And of course they're paying me. It's a job. I thought I explained all that to you."

"I know, I know. But I just couldn't believe it. And neither could the boys." Mary Lou turned, making an impatient clicking sound with her tongue. "Oh, where are those two, anyway? Gettin' them into a store that isn't videos or sportin' goods is just like pullin' a team of half-dead horses. . . ."

But just as Mary Lou began jumping up and down in front of me, the "boys" came into view — neat, dark-haired Ethan, of course, and just behind him, Roddy Fenton.

"He-e-e-y," Roddy exclaimed, while Ethan registered *his* reaction with a long, low whistle.

Roddy folded his arms and gazed at me, a baffled smile playing around his mouth, his eyes signaling mischief.

"What's the . . . outfit for?" Roddy wanted to know. "All those gold buttons. And the hat. I never saw you in a hat like that in my whole life, Glenda."

I gulped and glanced around me uncomfortably. I could have sworn Roddy had already formed the words *monkey suit* in his head before he stopped himself and simply said "outfit."

"Oh, you boys are so dumb," Mary Lou scolded. "Glenda looks real smart. They always put hats on fashion models, so they'll look *different*. That's what makes people sit up and take notice of them."

Roddy and Ethan stepped back as if to study me a little better. "Looks a little like my great-grandpop's derby," Roddy remarked. "Only his was black instead of orange."

"Pumpkin," I muttered irritably under my breath.

"Or sort of like Charlie Chaplin's," Ethan suggested, popping his eyes and giving himself a moustache by placing one finger across his upper lip.

"Very funny," I said, starting to walk away with Mary Lou at my heels. "Why did you bring those two clowns here, anyhow? Couldn't you just come on your own for once?"

"Oh, my goodness, don't be mad, Glenda," Mary Lou panted apologetically. "You know Ethan and I are seein' each other. And Roddy . . . he just doesn't *have* a girlfriend. Honestly, he was all excited when he heard about you bein' a model. I couldn't have kept him from comin' with us."

"Well," I said, "now you saw me, maybe you should all kind of . . . fade. I *am* supposed to be working, you know. I have to keep moving, talk to shoppers if they ask questions about the clothes, stuff like that."

But I just couldn't seem to shake Mary Lou *or* Roddy and Ethan, who kept following me as I started off again on my main-floor route. "I love the clothes you're wearin'," Mary Lou moaned admiringly. "I love the way they did your makeup. It's so . . . velvety. You know, I *always* wanted to be a model, Glenda. . . ."

I was sure the next thing Mary Lou was going to do would be to ask me to try to get her a job at Ballard's. But to my surprise, she seemed to have stopped in midsentence. "Oops," she exclaimed instead. "Maybe we *should* go. Here comes you know who."

Mary Lou could only have meant Patty. And, sure enough, there she stood just a short distance away, her dark eyes sullen because she had already seen Mary Lou and Ethan and Roddy.

Trying to act as professional as possible, and wanting to avoid any fireworks that might erupt between the two girls, I broke away from Mary Lou and approached Patty as though she were an interested shopper.

"Hi," I said, smiling a little stiffly. "The gang's all here."

"So I see," Patty replied tartly, keeping her voice low and talking between clenched teeth. "You look terrific, Glenda. But I'm not speaking to *her*. I'll wander over to the pantyhose counter till you get rid of them."

I nodded in agreement. But before Patty could even turn away, Mary Lou had rushed up to where we were standing. For some reason, she must have suddenly decided that a busy noontime on Ballard's main floor was a good place to try to become friends again with Patty.

"Hi!" Mary Lou greeted Patty breathlessly. "Isn't Glenda too fantastic?" She looked back at Ethan and Roddy. "Even the boys are impressed. But you know how *they* are. They have to gag everything up."

Patty just stood there glaring at Mary Lou. "Why

are you even talking to me?" she inquired coldly.

Mary Lou's pallid complexion went a few shades lighter. By now Ethan and Roddy had joined us. "What's up?" Roddy inquired innocently.

"Patty's angry at me," Mary Lou whined. She turned to Ethan imploringly. "Lately she's treated me just horribly. I don't know why she's bein' so mean."

"You don't *know*?" Patty challenged, curling her lip. She looked around, while the two boys continued to stare at the girls. "I'd be happy to tell you. But this is no place to discuss it."

Mary Lou seemed intent, though, on trying to make everything instantly right between them. She leaned toward Patty, touching her apologetically on the shoulder. But something went wrong. Maybe, as Patty instinctively drew away, Mary Lou's ring got caught in Patty's hair. It all happened so fast, I couldn't tell. The next moment Patty had her fingers in Mary Lou's hair. Mary Lou yowled, a high, sirenlike scream that seemed to go on and on. Then she dug her fingernails deeper into Patty's hair and neck.

"A-a-a-gh," Patty growled. "The nerve! The nerve of you. I'll get you for this, Mary Lou, so help me."

"Girls, girls!" A couple of saleswomen had rushed out from behind the jewelry counter and were tugging at furious little Patty. Meanwhile, Ethan struggled with Mary Lou, her arms flailing the air and her shrill screams still emerging, even though Patty had already let go of her.

I stood there, gaping in horror at my two friends

having a hair-pulling match on the main floor of Ballard's. I had nearly forgotten for the moment what *I* was doing there, when suddenly I felt myself being poked sharply from behind.

I turned, flashing with anger. The person who had poked me was Roddy Fenton.

"Listen, Glenda," he whispered hoarsely, "I think we should get you away from here."

Before I could answer, Roddy grabbed my hand, turned, and started running interference for me through the large crowd of onlookers that had gathered. He was right, of course. If Miss Oliver didn't even want my mother and Giselle in the store when I was working, what would she have said if she'd come upon a scene like this, with two of my school friends tearing at each other like a couple of tigresses? I was really impressed with how quick-thinking Roddy had been.

We kept right on moving, Roddy in the lead and me close behind him, until we reached the far back wall of the store where the service elevators were. Then Roddy let go my hand and I stood there huffing and puffing, fanning myself with my announcement card.

"I can't *believe* those two fighting that way," I panted. "I hope they're okay. You were right to pull me away, though. It could have cost me my job." I took a deep breath. "Thanks."

Roddy nodded but he didn't say anything. He just stood there, staring at me.

"*Now* what are you looking at?" I asked. The steadiness of his gaze was making me self-conscious. "I know you hate this outfit. You already made fun of it."

Roddy shrugged. "I don't hate it, Glenda. It's just that it's not . . . you."

"Oh," I murmured, wondering if that was a compliment. I also found myself wondering how come, every time Roddy and I found ourselves alone together lately, he stopped clowning and seemed to get so serious. It was as though he underwent a complete personality change. And it made me feel . . . different toward him.

"Well," I mumbled a little uncertainly, "I guess I'd better see about getting back on the floor pretty soon. Just in case anybody from upstairs comes looking for me."

Roddy sighed. "Yeah. Okay, Glenda. Lemme go first, though, and check out the scene. In case there are any dead bodies lying around."

I grinned. "Hope not. Oh, and Roddy, if you see Patty, um . . . make sure she's okay, huh? Mary Lou's got Ethan, so I'm not worried about *her*."

Roddy stood there hesitantly for a moment, looking as though he found my request to see how Patty was sort of peculiar. Then he waved an arm at me and melted into the crowd.

Chapter 16

"Glenda, honestly, is *that* all you're going to eat?" Patty inquired. She was poking her head inquisitively past Giselle's tray to mine as the three of us slid our lunches toward the cashier's counter in the school cafeteria.

I looked down at my tray. Even I couldn't help being a little surprised. Today was Monday, and my all-time favorite, tuna-noodle surprise, was the special, just as it was every Monday. But somehow I'd walked right past its once-heady aroma and chosen instead a pineapple ring topped with cottage cheese, sitting on a pale-green lettuce leaf.

"Patty's right," Giselle said, thumping me rather heartily on the back, "this is no time to start losing weight. What if they ask you to floor model again next Saturday?"

"*And*," Patty added, "don't forget about the big runway fashion show that's coming. You've got to keep up your strength, girl."

"Don't worry," I grinned. "I'll probably binge on an after-school snack when I get home. I always try to eat a light lunch. But then I go overboard a few hours later. How do you think I got this stunning fat-teen figure in the first place?"

"Never mind," Giselle remarked as we started for our usual table. "You really did look stunning on Saturday, Glenda. It just shows that big *can* be beautiful."

Yes, I thought, setting down my tray. But not *too* big. I couldn't help wondering if Giselle was feeling just a little sad these days at having had to let go of her own modeling career. How could she watch me doing something she had really loved and not feel the slightest twinge of envy? I was pretty sure *I* would have, if it had been the other way around.

The minute we sat down, kids started coming over to the table to talk. It was amazing how fast word had gotten around about my modeling over at the mall. Some of the school crowd must have wandered into Ballard's on Saturday and told others. So it turned out that, by the time I'd quit the floor late that afternoon, quite a few of them had seen me in one or more of the plus-teen outfits I'd modeled. And they wanted to know how it had all come about.

I kept nodding in Giselle's direction and telling them to ask her, because she deserved so much of the credit. But somehow they kept turning back to me. They just didn't seem to want to hear about Giselle's long-ago modeling career. Maybe they didn't believe it. Or maybe they were embarrassed because they were the same kids who'd slyly been making fun of her ever since she'd transferred to our school. And that made me feel even worse for Giselle.

Patty, on the other hand, seemed to be in pretty good spirits, in spite of her fight with Mary Lou on Saturday. Partly, I guessed, it was because Mary Lou was absent today. Nobody seemed to know why. But even if Mary Lou had one of her usual sniffly colds, how long could that last?

As soon as most of our table-hopping visitors had scattered, I hit Patty with the question that had been bothering me all weekend — what *was* she going to do about Mary Lou?

"Do?" Patty looked indignant. "Why, Glenda, I'm surprised. You were there. You saw what happened. She attacked me."

I shook my head. "Uh-uh, I don't think so. She was sort of trying to reach out to you. But then you ducked. And that's when your hair got tangled. . . ."

Patty closed her eyes and pursed her lips together stubbornly. "She *still* owes me an apology."

I exchanged glances with Giselle, who'd been listening carefully to the conversation while eating her lunch with her usual gusto.

"You know what?" I said, feeling the color rise in my cheeks. "You owe *me* an apology. Both you *and* Mary Lou. I'm still not sure those saleswomen who helped pull you two apart didn't make a report about what happened. If it ever gets back to Miss Oliver that friends of mine came in the store and had a hair-pulling and screaming match. . . ."

"Glenda's right," Giselle broke in, gently setting aside her polished-off lunch tray. "Ballard's is a class store. It could make things bad for Glenda. Just when she's getting started, too."

Patty flashed a look of annoyance at Giselle and then at me. "There you go again. Oh, you two are such buddy-buddies. Always standing up for each other. Nobody ever sees my side of things."

I gaped at Patty. She was getting really angry. I could see that she was still jealous over my friendship with Giselle.

"There *is* one person, though," Patty went on in a flaunting tone, "who's beginning to be nicer to me. *He* might even turn out to be a real good friend."

Giselle gave Patty a measured look. " 'He'? "

Patty pushed her lunch tray away and started to get up from the table. "Yes, 'he,' " she repeated. "Roddy Fenton, for both your information. He walked me all the way home from the mall on Saturday." The thrust of her chin, as she tilted it in the air, seemed to add the words, "So there!"

I couldn't suppress a flickering look in Giselle's direction. Because I'd already told her how, after Roddy had spirited me away from the scene of the fight at Ballard's, I'd asked him to make sure Patty was okay.

Patty, of course, would have been furious if she'd known that Roddy, who'd never especially liked her, had simply been doing me a favor. "Um, where are you going?" I asked, as Patty suddenly swept her lunch tray up into her arms.

"For ice cream," Patty retorted sharply. "And I don't know if I'm coming back."

"Wow," Giselle commented as she looked after Patty's small but determined retreating figure. "Was she always such a spitfire?"

I poked what was left of my cottage cheese into the hole in the pineapple slice. Somehow even that tiny lunch had been a little too much for me. "She's having a rough time lately," I admitted. "But I can't worry anymore about her and Mary Lou. For all I care, they can both be mad at me. I'm just so nervous all the time thinking about the . . . the fashion show."

"Oh, don't be," Giselle advised warmly. "If the store likes the new plus-teen clothing line and the fashion coordinator likes you, you can't miss. You'll be in it."

"That's what I'm worried about."

Giselle's eyes widened. "Why, Glenda? You did fine on Saturday. Floor modeling is a really hard way to break in, all on your own in a crowd of crazy shoppers. A fashion show is much easier."

"I don't see how," I sighed. "Miss Oliver says you have to model about six different outfits in an hour. You have to make split-second changes backstage. You have to know your place in the lineup and be able to take off a coat or a jacket without breaking your stride. You even have to know the exact number of steps to the end of the runway."

"So?" Giselle said, unimpressed. "We can practice. I'll help you. I'll come to your house, and we can time the changes, complete with hair and makeup. We'll get it all down to a science. It'll be fun."

I shook my head. "And there'll be all those other models in the changing room. Skinny ones, with great bodies. Teens who look like . . . what teens ought to look like. I'll feel like such a klutz getting into my oversize togs alongside them. And when the show starts and we all parade out onto the runway . . ." I could hardly finish painting the picture that had been forming in my mind. "Then I'll really stand out from the crowd."

Giselle gave me a searching look, just as the warning bell rang for the end of our lunch period. We started to get our things together.

"Glenda," Giselle said, emptying my tray and sliding it under hers, "you *wanted* to be a plus-teen model. You said it would make you feel that weighing twelve pounds more than you did last summer wasn't the biggest disaster in your life, because you'd actually be turning it into an advantage. Remember?"

"I know," I murmured. "But now, I want . . . more."

"More?" Giselle stood up and glanced down at me. "More what? There are tons of teenage girls in this country who come in all shapes and sizes. And you're doing a great job of showing them how nice they can look in clothes that are made for *real* people. You're doing the best you can and being the best you can be. Isn't that enough for you?"

I gave Giselle a woeful look. Her words made me feel ashamed because I realized how much better off I was — as an overweight teen — than she was. There was something inside me, though, that was driving my discontent. I didn't dare say the words out loud to Giselle. But what I wanted to be, instead of a plus-teen model, was a *normal* teen model. Or, if I couldn't be that, just a normal teenage girl.

Chapter 17

"What about lunch?" Giselle wanted to know. "We could have Greek food. Or Chinese. Or Japanese. That's probably the *least* fattening. Raw fish and rice, with some slivers of veggie."

"Sushi," I remarked, looking doubtful. "If *you* want it. Doesn't matter to me."

Giselle shrugged and grinned. "Let's go up to the international food floor and look around. Who knows, maybe we'll end up with a hamburger or a hot dog after all."

I nodded and we headed for the up escalator. It was Sunday afternoon, the day after my second Saturday of floor modeling at Ballard's, and Giselle and I were in the Havenhurst Shopping Mall hunting for shoes for me. So far I'd bought one pair.

"I can't believe I took a whole size smaller," I said as we were wafted toward the parade of food stands that sold everything from English fish-and-chips to Israeli falafel, their odors blending into a steamy mishmash that didn't smell like any one thing in particular.

Giselle took a sniff of all this cookery and looked

blissful. "I've been telling you all along, Glenda, that you were losing weight. And when you lose weight, it shows up in your shoe size just like in everything else you wear. But, no, you have to keep on being stubborn and refuse to get on a scale. You haven't weighed yourself in ten days at least."

I shook my head. "I *can't* have lost that much. They must have put the wrong size on those shoes. I just hope they don't turn out to be tight."

But even though I wouldn't admit it, I probably had lost a few pounds lately. And yesterday, Miss Oliver had noticed it as she'd ordered the next smaller plus-teen size off the rack for me.

"Don't go skinny on me just now, da-r-r-ling," she'd cautioned, giving me a light warning pat on the hip. "We put you into the big runway show in two weeks. So keep up a good appetite."

That was the moment when I'd learned for sure that I was going to be in Ballard's late-fall showing of next spring's fashions, as the only model for the new plus-teen clothing line. And my pulse had started racing, my head throbbing, in a mixture of delight and apprehension.

"So . . ." Giselle said, licking her lips as we started to stroll past the different food offerings. Each stand faced the large semicircle of cafeteria-style tables that swept around one entire end of the mall's second floor. "Should we get a table first or buy our stuff first? Did you decide if you want Japanese or not? What do you think about something to drink?"

Giselle's preoccupation with food and eating had really begun to get to me lately. At the moment, we were standing in front of one of the Greek booths, piled high with stacks of pita bread and tall, upright spits of roasting meat.

"Listen," I said abruptly, "I'll go get a table. You get whatever you like. And just bring me a Greek salad. Okay?"

Giselle gave me a slightly startled look as I dashed away into the maze of tables, clutching the shoes I'd bought. Miss Oliver had told me to get two pairs of miniheeled pumps, one in taupe and one in bone, and suggested I have them well broken in for the runway show. "Sore feet will make you move badly," she'd advised. "Best to be comfortable. You can walk miles on a runway."

I began zigzagging my way toward an empty table I'd spotted in a quiet part of the eating area. My mind was still focused on the second pair of shoes I had to get, plus some extra pantyhose, a couple of new shades of makeup, and some more hair spray. Suddenly, I felt a tug at the strap of my shoulder bag.

Grabbing hard at my bag, I turned around in alarm. You couldn't be too careful in the mall. There were tricky characters who hung around just waiting for kids and other unwary shoppers who were too casual with their purses.

"Glenda!" a bunch of voices cried out in unison.

I looked down at the table I'd just brushed past in my haste. Familiar faces were turned up to me — Mary

Lou and Ethan, Patty and . . . Roddy. It was Roddy who'd hooked his finger into the shoulder strap of my bag. In fact, he still hadn't let go.

"Join us," Mary Lou cried out happily. "It's such a surprise seein' you here, Glenda. You all alone?"

In a flash, the latest goings-on among my friends were revealed to me. I could see that Mary Lou and Patty had made up their spat. It must have only just happened on the weekend, because Mary Lou hadn't been in school all week. I had a hunch, too, that Patty's being partnered by Roddy — as she now appeared to be — had helped soften her feelings of boyfriend envy toward Mary Lou.

"Yeah," Roddy repeated, still tugging at my purse strap and starting to get up from his chair, "Sit down, Glenda." He seemed uneasy, his face a little pale. "You eating lunch? Want me to get you something?"

I looked around the table. Remains of hamburgers, Cokes, and other partly eaten snacks sat at each place.

"Um, no," I stammered. "That is, I *am* eating, but Giselle's bringing it. I have to go get a table." I surveyed the four occupied places. "There wouldn't be room, anyhow."

Patty's dark eyes sought mine. "We could all move to a different one," she suggested, a little halfheartedly, I thought. I could hardly blame her. Since our tiff in the school cafeteria on Monday, she hadn't been on the best of terms with Giselle and me.

"Uh-uh," I said quickly. "I think I see Giselle coming. I'd better get us a place."

I waved my hand and made off as gracefully as I could.

But as I slumped into a chair at the table I'd been heading for, I found myself strangely shaken. The encounter I'd just had with my old friends left me feeling that a distance had been growing between us ever since I'd started my modeling assignments. Nor could I help wondering if there was anything brewing these days between Patty and Roddy — like a possible romance. Even if there was, I told myself, what did I care? They were both free to do as they liked.

On the other hand, how come Roddy had acted so jumpy and anxious just now when he'd caught hold of me? And why had he seemed so unwilling to let me go? Did he think he was being disloyal to me in some way? Did he have a guilty conscience?

Just like every other boy I'd ever known, Roddy Fenton was turning out to be a riddle to me.

"There's a name for what's happening to you, Glenda," my mother said, shaking her finger at me.

It was later that evening, and I was padding around my room picking up pants, skirts, sweaters, shoes, and other articles of clothing. They lay all over the bed, floor, desk, and chairs in complete disarray, along with brushes, combs, hair spray, and makeup.

"I'm cleaning up," I groaned as I slowly hooked a T-shirt off the floor with my big toe and hoisted it onto the bed. "Just give me a chance. I'm tired."

"Of course you're tired," my mother said, picking

her way deeper into the room. "You're tired because you're undernourished. A Greek salad for lunch and a low-calorie soda for dinner. What kind of eating is that? The next thing I know you'll be developing a classic case of anorexia, refusing to eat altogether and turning into a pathetic little bag of bones."

I brushed away a clump of hair that was hanging in my eyes. "Oh, that's the most ridiculous thing I ever heard," I declared. "I'm tired because of the run-through for the fashion show that Giselle and I did after we got back from the mall this afternoon. We were working with a stopwatch, trying to make complete costume changes in two minutes, with hair and makeup all perfect. It was exhausting. I don't see how I'm going to get through the show at all."

My mother folded up a few pieces of clothing that had been lying across my little flowered-chintz boudoir chair and sat down in it herself.

"Now, now," she said soothingly, "don't panic, Glenda. You'll make all the changes in time just like everybody else in the show. Maybe I could arrange with Miss Oliver to stay backstage with you and help you."

"No!" I shrieked. "Don't you dare."

"All right, all right," my mother replied hastily, her hands flying up defensively in front of her face.

I plopped down on the bed opposite her and blew out a pent-up breath of exasperation. "That's all I'd need. The 'fat girl' with her mother, in front of all those great-looking size-three models. There were a few of them in the dressing room with me last Saturday getting ready to floor model. You should have seen the way they looked at me."

"Only because they're ignorant," my mother said. "I was reading only the other day that there are 50 percent *more* overweight adolescents in the United States today than there were ten years ago. Somebody has to model clothes for young people who have a little more flesh on them than a . . . bean pole."

"Well," I murmured, looking down at my bare feet, "I'm not sure it ought to be me. I thought I'd be so happy to be a fashion model — any kind. But no matter what you say, it's still a skinny person's world."

"There you go again," my mother said, her voice rising. "I can just read the handwriting on the wall. A girl like you gets a modeling job, decides it isn't glamorous enough for her to be showing extra-size fashions, gets a crazy idea that she ought to lose a little weight, then a little more, and a little more. She stops eating sensibly and pretty soon . . ."

I plunged my fingers into my hair and raked it back sharply from my face.

"Will you *ever* stop!" I exclaimed. "Don't you think I *know* that I'll never be a size three? If I'm not eating much lately it's only because I'm nervous about the fashion show. Every time I think of getting up on that runway in front of a whole roomful of people, all I know is that I want to look the . . . the very best I can."

My mother got up from her chair and gave me a doubtful glance. "Hummph," she remarked. "That excuse for not eating doesn't make any kind of sense to me. You always used to eat *more* when you got nervous or upset about something."

I leaned over to pick up a shoe that was lying at the foot of my bed. "I know," I growled impatiently at my mother. "But I was never a fat-teen model in a Ballard's department-store fashion show before, either."

Suddenly my father, newspaper in hand, was standing in the doorway of my room.

"I heard screams coming from here a moment ago," he said wearily. "What's going on now, may I ask?"

My mother gave him a resentful look. "Nothing important, Harold," she said bitterly. "Only that your daughter is turning herself into an anorexic before our very eyes. And she won't even admit it!" With that, she whipped out a handkerchief, dabbed vigorously at her nose and eyes, and stalked past him out of the room.

My father stood facing me. "An anorexic?" He blinked a couple of times. "Is that what I think it is?"

I jumped off the bed and went up to him, looking deep into his eyes. "Believe me, Daddy," I said imploringly, "that's *not* what I am. I'm okay. Just a little uptight these days. But okay."

My father's face relaxed, and a faint smile began to play across his lips. I threw my arms around him, and he started to rub my back comfortingly, the newspaper still rustling in his hand.

"There, there," he said warmly, his moustache tickling my neck. "There's my girl, my Glenda."

I hugged him tighter, happy to have at least one parent who seemed to understand the way I was feeling.

Chapter 18

It was early Saturday morning, the day of the big runway fashion show at Ballard's. Dazed and droopy from an almost sleepless night, I stood gazing at myself in the bathroom mirror. My eyelids were puffy, my tongue was coated, my teeth were dingy, and my hair — which I'd carefully washed and blown-dry before bedtime — was definitely *wrinkled.*

Furiously, I dragged a comb through the tangles and clumps it had worked itself into during my damp and restless night. I'd learned from my floor-modeling experience how to pull, tease, and spray my hair. But today it was totally unmanageable. And there'd be no time to wash it again before I had to be at the store for a full rehearsal.

"Glenda, was that you I heard groaning?" My mother was standing at the bathroom door in her pale-blue furry bathrobe. "You're not . . . sick?" she inquired, her eyes widening with alarm. "Is there something I can get you?"

"Yes," I mumbled, giving her a saggy look. "Ice cubes, bicarbonate, peroxide."

"Ice cubes, bicarb . . ." my mother repeated. She dashed over to me and clapped one hand to my forehead. "You're hot, I think. Oh, Glenda, you can't have a fever *today*."

"I don't," I said, not sounding all that reassuring. "I need the ice for my puffy eyes. And the bicarbonate and peroxide for a paste to whiten my teeth. Those are tips Giselle gave me. They really work, too."

My mother looked baffled for a moment. Then she sprang into action, rushing off to the kitchen for the ice and bicarbonate, to her own bathroom for the peroxide.

"You're sure about this?" she remarked doubtfully, returning with a bowl of ice cubes and the other items I'd asked for.

"Yes, yes," I murmured, putting moist cotton pads on the ice cubes to chill and mixing the paste for my teeth.

"Well," my mother said, slowly backing out of the room, "I'll go get dressed so I can drive you to the store. Is there any chance you'll eat some breakfast first?" There was a definite note of insinuation in her voice. Ever since she and I had argued almost two weeks ago, when she'd accused me of turning into an anorexic, food had been a touchy subject between us.

"Sure, I'll have breakfast," I said, trying to sound hearty and please her. "Um, yogurt, I think."

I could hear my mother tsk-tsking in disapproval as she padded down the hall. Plain, low-fat yogurt wasn't *her* idea of a proper breakfast for a fat-teen model.

Of course, I still didn't know for sure if I'd lost weight. Because I'd continued to refuse to get on the scale. Maybe I *had* dropped a pound or two in the past few weeks. But so what? I still felt like Fat Glenda, plenty plump enough to do my job on the runway in the big Ballard's fashion show.

About an hour later, my mother dropped me off at the employees' entrance to the store, blew me a wistful kiss, and drove away. She'd be coming back this afternoon to see the show, of course. But I'd finally trained her — after two Saturdays of floor modeling and one, last week, of preparations for the runway show — not to come inside with me and hover like an uneasy shadow until Miss Oliver had to ask her to leave.

I felt calm and composed as I entered the still-empty store and made my way to the up escalator. But the moment I stepped off it into the misses and teens apparel section on the second floor, my nerves began to tingle. A large area had been cleared of clothing racks, counters, and cash registers, and transformed into a roped-off seating area for the fashion show. The runway itself sliced through the two banks of empty chairs that would later fill up with three or four hundred invited guests, all of them equipped with X-ray eyes.

I stopped and stared at the raised platform on which I'd be parading with the other models. It *was* narrow, only just wide enough for two people walking side by side. And the three-foot drop to the ground looked surprisingly steep. With a shudder, I imagined "going dizzy," as Miss Oliver had put it — weaving, stumbling, and hurtling into the laps of the horrified and giggling onlookers.

"H-h-h-n-g!" One hand clutching my throat, I let out an involuntary gasp.

"Something the matter?" a crisp young voice behind me inquired. I turned and recognized two of the teen models, the "size threes," who had been at last Saturday's fitting session for the fashion show. One of them was named Brooke and the other was Cyndi — "with a y and an i," she'd informed me. But I couldn't remember which girl was which.

"Um, the runway," I gurgled hoarsely, trying to clear my voice. "It seems so . . . high."

The two girls arched their eyebrows and exchanged glances, but they didn't say anything. At the same moment, Miss Oliver appeared just outside the fitting-room entrance.

"Young ladies," she called out, "please not to stand around making empty talk. We have no time to waste."

Inside the fitting room, seven or eight misses-size models were already standing about in various stages of dress. A bevy of "pin ladies," fitters and seamstresses with pincushions on their wrists and rows of straight pins in their mouths, kneeled, stooped, and flurried around the tall, slinky models.

"You!" said a deep-voiced fitting lady with glasses

perched low on her nose as she approached me briskly. "Are you Glenda, for the plus-teen line?"

I nodded.

"Come," she said. "The manufacturer just sent a bunch of new spring samples we didn't expect. Silk, real linen, leather like butter. Gorgeous stuff. We're trying to get another plus-teen model in for today. But so far she's a no-show."

Near the partly curtained alcove where I started to get undressed, a couple of women stood ironing the folds out of the clothes, fresh from their delivery boxes.

"We'll try this one first," the fitter said, coming toward me. "It's a natural with your hair color." She was holding up a short tangerine-leather skirt and a chalk-white top, waist length and trimmed with matching bands of tangerine leather. "I'm Trudi," she added, as she slipped the skirt on over my head. "Heard you already did some modeling on this line. Should fit you perfect."

"Yes, twice. Informal floor modeling," I mumbled, smothered for the moment in the darkness of the softly lined skirt. Then the skirt slipped down onto my hips, and Trudi knelt behind me to work the zipper at the back.

"Now what's this?" she muttered, a note of irritation creeping into her voice. Something was probably wrong with the zipper. I already knew that broken zippers were a nightmare that haunted all models and dressers, especially in runway shows, where timing was everything.

Suddenly, Trudi got to her feet, came around in front of me, placed her hands at my waist, and began to swirl my skirt loosely back and forth.

"You said you was Glenda, right?"

"Of course," I told her, craning my head around to try to see the back of the skirt. "Is the zipper broken?"

"No it ain't," she replied in a grinding tone. "Zipper's fine." To prove it, she grabbed the skirt again and slid it half way around me, easily bringing the back to the front so I could see it. "Zipper's fine," she repeated. "But you ain't."

I stared down at the too-big skirt and then at Trudi. "Well," I said almost indignantly, "let's try a smaller size." I was going to add that Miss Oliver had had to do that a couple of weeks ago. But then I figured I'd better not.

Trudi folded her arms across her chest and peered at me over the tops of her glasses. "There ain't no smaller size, missy," she replied grimly. "This *is* the smallest. It's a line for fat kids, remember? And *you*," she added accusingly, "don't weigh enough."

The next moment she turned away from me in disgust and started across the room, calling out in a voice heavy with doom, "Miss Oliver, we got a problem here."

Chapter 19

It was two o'clock. Standing in the lineup ready to make my first fashion-show entrance, I could hear the hum and twitter of voices beyond the curtained area that led from the dressing room to the runway steps.

"I'm okay," I told myself, breathing deep into my abdomen as Miss Oliver had coached us. "I won't get dizzy. I won't trip. I'll remember how many steps to take before I show the jacket lining, where to turn, how to get back. . . ."

We'd had two complete run-throughs since the morning, complete with bright lights, music, and the voice of the commentator describing the highlights of each model's costume and the name of the designer or manufacturer. And now, at last, it was "show time."

Directly in front of me stood Cyndi and, in front of her, Brooke. I'd finally learned which girl was which. They were both teen, or junior-size, models with streaked and tangled blonde hair and stunning "petite" figures. I was the only plus-size model in the show because, as Trudi had expected, the one the store had ordered from an agency had never turned up. Behind me was a string of misses-size models, all five feet eight or over, slim and gorgeous.

"Oops," I squeaked, as Cyndi took an unexpected step backward and nearly threw me off balance.

She turned, looked at me blandly, and murmured, "Sorry." Even though she was supposed to have lots of experience doing runway shows, she seemed as jumpy as a racehorse at the starting gate.

Suddenly, Miss Oliver came down the line for one last inspection, stiffening a collar here, fluffing a sleeve there. When she came to me, she smacked my hip firmly with the palm of her hand. "The padding is good, yes, da-r-r-ling?"

I nodded, blushing slightly with the embarrassment I'd been feeling ever since Trudi had announced my "problem" to the entire dressing room. It was ridiculous. But the fitters and Miss Oliver had decided that there was no way I could model even the smallest sizes in the plus-teen line unless I wore a thick cotton wrapping under my clothes. So one of the sewing ladies had quickly run up on her machine a sort of short half slip that looked like it was made out of a mattress pad. The secret I'd been keeping even from myself was out. I'd been dropping pounds — quite a lot of them — and was now too "thin" to be a fat-teen model. But there was no one else to take my place, and the show had to go on.

"Naughty girl," Miss Oliver remarked, wagging a finger at me as she started past. "Fat or skinny, a model must stay as she is supposed to be. We cannot use you again, da-r-r-ling, if you do not get a bit more plump."

Cyndi, of course, had heard Miss Oliver's words and leaned forward to whisper something in Brooke's ear. I felt a deep stab of dislike for both girls. If they thought I was trying to get down to a size three to compete with them, they didn't need to worry. The real disappointment for me was that, without even trying too hard, I'd slimmed down to the best silhouette I'd probably ever have. And now — just when I wanted to look my very best — I'd had to submit to being artificially made *fatter* so I could be the token "plus-teen" in the fashion show.

"We're on!" somebody whispered. And to a rising volume of jaunty soft-rock music, the line in front of me began to move forward and onto the runway. Spotlights, more blinding than I'd remembered from rehearsals, dazzled me as I began to walk, count, turn, and do all the movements that I'd been taught, like a mindless but obedient mechanical doll.

Somewhere out there in the audience were my mother and father — yes, my father had actually given up his golf game to be present — and Giselle. I'd managed to wangle an extra ticket for her. But most of the by-invitation-only audience was made up of "preferred" charge customers, plus a sprinkling of fashion experts, merchandising people, and designers and manufacturers.

Waves of applause rose and fell as the special features of each model's outfit were announced. I thought I heard some extra-loud clapping and even a faint whistle or two from the crowd when I had my big moment to twirl and display the clothes I was wearing. Then it was back to the dressing room to be seized by the dressers assigned to us, ripped out of our clothes, and zipped into new ones. Our makeup was retouched, our hair was recombed, and we were pushed into the lineup again, ready to reappear on the runway.

After the second or third outfit, I began to feel like I was caught in a giant revolving door. It was dress, model, undress; dress, model, undress. If I or anybody else dared to miss a beat, everything would tumble down around us like a house of cards. I still hadn't been able to spot my parents or Giselle in the audience. But that was probably just as well. Their tense, eager, or worried smiles would only have made me more nervous. In the bright glare of the stage lights, I had all I could do to concentrate on my assigned movements in the lineup behind Cyndi.

I was on my fifth outfit, the beautiful tangerine-leather skirt with the tangerine-trimmed white-leather top. Only one more outfit to go, and the show would be over. Each time I'd changed clothes, I'd had to check my underpadding to make sure it was still in place. Since it had been run up on the sewing machine at the last minute, there was no time to put a zipper in it. So it was fastened with straight pins, carefully inserted on the underside of the material so as not to show through and also not to stick me.

Once again we stood in the lineup, ready to go on, breathing hard from the exertion of the latest costume change. As we waited, Cyndi kept turning around to glance at me and finally said, "I'm just crazy about that leather you're wearing. I can't *believe* it only comes in plus sizes. I'd love it for me."

"I know," I replied, amazed that she had actually started a semifriendly conversation. "Even I couldn't wear it without this . . . padding."

Cyndi smirked. "It would be totally wasted on a really fat girl."

I lowered my eyelids in silent response. Her snobbery, which I should have expected, was infuriating. With all the great clothes that were made for skinny people, she didn't have to be so grudging of a few really nice ones designed for the fatties of this world.

The next moment we were off again, onto the runway and into the waiting crowd. I was counting steps, keeping the proper distance from Cyndi just in front of me, watching her get ready to unbutton the skirt of the abbreviated playsuit she was wearing so she could display the hot pants underneath, when she suddenly came to an abrupt halt.

At the same time, she leaned sharply forward, so far over in fact that she seemed to be touching the floor with one hand, as though she was groping for something. There was a rising hum from the crowd. What was going on?

With only a split second to either stop myself dead or detour around her, I tried to break or adjust my stride. But I couldn't do either. I had too much momentum. Without meaning to or wanting to, I bumped hard into Cyndi's stalled and stooping figure. The next instant both of us went sprawling.

Triggerfast, somebody had turned up the volume of the music, probably to cover the gasps of surprise and rising titters of laughter from the audience. "You clumsy . . . *ox*," Cyndi hissed, as we both began hastily scrambling to our feet. "I'll get you for this. I lost my contact lens. Now I'll *never* find it."

"How should *I* know why you stopped short?" I retorted in a stinging tone. "It was your own fault."

Closing one eye and winking crazily because of the distortion in her vision, Cyndi wheeled around in front of me, gave me a leer, and staggered punch-drunkenly down the runway. Without missing a beat, the fashion-show commentator softened the music again and her voice came back over the microphone with, "And next, from the plus-teen line of one of our most forward-looking American designers. . . ."

I knew this was the signal for me to begin the poses and circular movements I'd been instructed to do to show off the lines, front and back, of the tangerine-leather outfit. Riffs of laughter were still coming from the audience. But I ignored them. We'd been told that, no matter what hitches developed on the runway, we were to keep on going as though nothing had happened. And that was exactly what I was doing. So why was the noise from the audience mounting steadily into fresh peals of mirth?

Determinedly, I continued my promenade to the T-shaped end of the runway, which was our turnaround, the laughter increasing all around me. It was getting harder to hide the shaky, almost sickly feeling growing inside me. But now, at least, I was on my return route. And striding toward me was the figure of the misses-size model whose place in the lineup was just behind mine.

She was tall and had a glaring, defiant look. I'd never spoken to her. In fact, I'd only seen her for the first time today. But to my surprise she spoke to me, clearly and sharply, as we passed each other. "Better speed it up baby," she mouthed through clenched teeth, barely moving her lips. "Your underwear is coming down."

Underwear! Underwear? Horrified, I lowered my eyes as far as my thighs. Sure enough, something white was descending from beneath the hem of my short tangerine-leather skirt. Now that I'd seen it, I could *feel* it moving as well.

Desperately, I clapped my hands firmly to my sides, hoping to somehow hold things in place until I was off the runway. But it was too late.

The pins that had fastened the white-cotton underpadding for my oversize skirt must have come loose when I'd stumbled over Cyndi and begun wriggling around on the floor, trying to get up as fast as I could. Or maybe the pins had started to loosen even sooner, during the last couple of frantic costume changes back in the dressing room.

In any case, the embarrassing-looking "stuffing" designed to turn me into a fat teen was now beginning to slip toward my knees. Soon it would be at my calves. Next it would be at my ankles. All I could do was to keep on telling myself that, with a few more steps, I'd be off the runway — forever.

Yes, forever! Let the crowd continue to rock with amusement. What did that have to do with me? Because, all at once, I knew with certainty that I wasn't coming back. I didn't *need* to be a fashion model anymore. I'd suddenly realized that, in a very short time, I had become a new and different Glenda. And I didn't have anything to be ashamed of.

Maybe I was too thin to be a fat model and not thin enough to be a skinny model. But I was proud of how I looked and pleased with who I was.

Buoyed by my newborn feeling of triumph, I had a bold inspiration. Reaching down around my knees, I wrenched the strip of mattress padding loose, raised it high above my head, and twirled it in the air like a banner.

To my astonishment, the laughter of the audience faded abruptly only to transform itself into a huge burst of applause — a kind of roar of approval. Its satisfying sound reverberated in my ears all the way back to the dressing room.

Chapter 20

The main event of the season, the Ballard's runway fashion show, was almost over. In a few minutes, all of the models would be drifting back to the dressing room. Although drooping with exhaustion, they'd be muttering about all the big and little things that had gone wrong. They'd probably be making cutting remarks, too, about the clothes, the commentator, the audience, and mostly each other. But I wasn't going to stay around for any of that. I'd already wiped off my makeup, climbed into my jeans, and packed my bag with the shoes, pantyhose, cosmetics, and other accessories I'd brought along.

At first, Miss Oliver had been in a stormy mood, angry at both the fitter who hadn't pinned my padding on carefully enough and at me for needing it in the first place. But she was calmer now as she clocked me out.

"Maybe you'll come back to us, da-r-r-ling, for the spring promotion," she even suggested. "*If* you are plump once again. But this time," her widening eyes glittered with an unspoken threat, "you must promise to stay so.

"As for that other trouble," Miss Oliver went on, tilting her blonde head toward Cyndi, who sat moping at the other end of the dressing room, "it was most unprofessional of our Miss Cyndi to stop on the runway as she did. For this I do not hold you responsible."

Cyndi, too, had not gone back into the fashion-show lineup after the accident that she had caused. She was waiting around in the dressing room, though, for her friend Brooke. And, aside from casting a few murderous glances in my direction, she had done nothing but wail about her lost contact lens and threaten to sue the store if it wasn't found in wearable condition once the runway was cleared.

As I slipped out the dressing-room door, a feeling of immense relief swept over me. I didn't have the slightest regret about all that I was leaving behind. Did Miss Oliver actually think I'd purposely sit down and eat myself fat again so I could once more be a plus-teen model? Wasn't that almost exactly what had happened to Giselle, whose childhood career as a chubby toddler had led to her being a blimp-size adolescent? With an example like that in front of me, I'd have to be pretty dim not to learn *something*.

Since Miss Oliver had warned us to keep our relatives and friends away from the dressing room after the show, I'd arranged to meet my parents and Giselle at the frozen-yogurt shop, which was located in the mall a short distance from Ballard's. As I headed for the down escalator leading to the busy main floor, I noticed that nobody even glanced my way. Once out of my model's togs and stage makeup, I was just an ordinary "civilian." What a difference from that day, weeks ago, when I'd descended this very escalator with Miss Oliver, wearing my "monkey suit" and feeling like an overdressed curiosity, about to be tossed to the crowd.

I was still reveling in the pleasure of being a nobody — especially a thinner nobody than I'd ever been before — when a hand clutched mine as it rested on the escalator banister. Who would have the nerve to do something like that on purpose unless it was someone who knew me? I turned sharply. Standing directly behind me, probably watching me the whole time I'd been quietly basking in my newfound privacy and freedom, was Roddy Fenton.

"Oh!" I exclaimed, partly annoyed, partly relieved. "It's you."

Roddy grinned and moved down a step to stand alongside me, so that we got off the escalator together.

"What are you doing in the store?" I asked. "Are the other kids here, too? Is Patty with you?"

"Nope," Roddy replied, looking mysterious.

Beginning to feel a little jumpy, I started to thread my way toward the nearest exit. "Don't tell me, Roddy," I said, talking to him over my shoulder as I hurried on, "that you're wandering around Ballard's all by yourself on a Saturday afternoon. That doesn't sound like you."

Roddy gripped my elbow suddenly to steer me away from a knot of people I'd nearly bumped into.

"Well," I persisted, "answer me, can't you? Or is it some kind of secret?"

"No secret," Roddy replied in a straightforward manner. "I guess I came to see you."

"See *me*? How did you know I'd be . . . ?" A horrible thought struck me. Could Roddy possibly have been at the fashion show? *Roddy?*

We had already reached the large, enclosed entrance area between the inside and outside doors of the store. "You aren't coming from the . . . the show?" I ventured.

Roddy just stood there nodding faintly.

"Oh, no!" I exclaimed, my voice rising with indignation, as all of the embarrassment I'd felt for most of those last minutes on the runway washed over me again. Before I could stop myself, I actually threw my carryall bag at Roddy so that it hit him softly in the chest before he caught it. "You were in the audience? You saw . . . the whole thing?" I narrowed my eyes at him. "How'd you get in, anyway?"

"Invitation," Roddy replied jauntily, tossing my bag in the air as though it were a basketball and leaping up to catch it.

I suppressed a smile of disbelief. "*You* got an invitation to the Ballard's fashion show? Oh, come on, Roddy."

"Honest." Roddy raised his right hand solemnly. "Well, all right, my mom did. See, she practically refurnished our whole house last spring on her Ballard's charge account. So she was on the . . . guest list."

I bobbed my head knowingly. "But *she* didn't go to the fashion show. You took the invitation and went instead."

Roddy shrugged. "Well, yeah. Sort of."

I backed away slightly. "Why? So you could report to Patty and the others?" I stuck my arm out. "Give me my stuff, Roddy. I have to go meet my parents and Giselle. . . ."

But Roddy only shifted my bag to his other shoulder. "You've got it all wrong, Glenda. Like I said, I came to see *you*. Period."

I thought for a moment about the whistles and extraloud clapping I'd heard in the audience when I'd made my first appearance on the runway. But it was still hard for me to believe that Roddy was being sincere. "Maybe you came so you could admire me in all those goofy outfits. Especially that . . . last one you just saw me in."

Roddy took a few steps closer to me to get out of the stream of people entering and leaving the store. "Have it your own way if you won't believe me, Glenda. Patty told me you already have a boyfriend. Some guy named Justin that you met last summer. So it's probably no use my asking you if you'd like to go around to the video store with me this afternoon and pick out . . ."

I stared at Roddy, who'd been speaking more and more rapidly. Suddenly, I was in a state of shock. "Patty told you *what*?"

Roddy set my bag down on the floor and actually

raised both arms in a gesture of self-defense. "What did I say now to get you so upset?" he inquired innocently.

I ran my fingers through my hair. "I'm not upset with *you*, Roddy. At least I don't think so. Did Patty really tell you I still have this . . . boyfriend?"

Roddy arched his neck uneasily. "She said that was probably the reason why you didn't write back to me last summer. She said you were going around with this . . . pretty smooth guy."

What had Patty been trying to do, I wondered. Did she want Roddy to think I was still in touch with Justin in order to make me look good? Or was she trying to improve her own chances with Roddy?

I'd never known Patty to be tricky enough to tell an outright lie. But maybe Mary Lou's romance with Ethan had made her desperate. She'd been jealous of so many things these last months, including Giselle's friendship with me and my so-called modeling career.

"Smooth guy?" I muttered, in a mocking tone to Roddy. *Slippery character is more like it*, I told myself silently.

Giselle had been right when she'd called Justin just another boy with a short-term memory. I could see now that whether I was fat, thin, or in-between, it wouldn't have made any difference. Yet, until Roddy had mentioned his name a moment ago, Justin's silence had continued to trouble me. It was only now — for the first time since we'd said good-bye on that final day at the inn — that I realized that Justin no longer had the power to hurt me, not the least bit. The *boing* in the pit of my stomach whenever I thought of him just didn't . . . boing anymore.

I picked up my carryall bag and slung it over my shoulder. "So what were you saying about the video store?" I asked Roddy.

His mouth stretched into a broad grin. "Meet me there around five? You pick the flick. No horror stuff if you don't want any."

We started for the doors leading out into the mall. "Um, so where are we going to watch this famous video that I get to choose?" I asked. "Your house or mine?"

Roddy dashed on ahead to hold the door open for me. "Wherever you say, Glenda," he replied, making a low, sweeping bow. "You decide."

Chapter 21

Giselle was waiting for me in the frozen-yogurt shop when I got there. She had taken a booth for four, and the menu of dessert concoctions pictured in wild, Day-Glo colors was spread out on the table in front of her. My parents were nowhere in sight.

"Oh . . . Glenda." Giselle got up, her expression full of concern, and reached both arms out to me. "What a *shame* about that little creep in front of you. Your mother was *so* angry. She and your father stopped in Ballard's to buy something. But I think actually your father wanted to try to calm her down before she saw you. Never mind, though. You were still the hit of the show. In your own way."

"Well, um, thanks." I returned Giselle's hug and slid quickly into the booth. "There's really nothing for my mother — or anybody else — to be upset about, though."

Giselle took her seat opposite me. "I'm so relieved you're taking such a good attitude, Glenda. It's the sign of a real professional. I'm not surprised they had to pad you, though," she sighed. "I *knew* you were getting too thin. Why did you do it, Glenda?"

Giselle's question hit me right between the eyes. "*Why*?" I could hardly conceal the surprise, faintly tinged with outrage, that I felt. "Why not? Was I supposed to go on stuffing myself, even when I didn't feel like eating, just so I could look like some kind of a circus freak — "

I stopped myself abruptly. What was I saying? Would Giselle think I was talking about looking like *her*? It was so easy for people who'd had a little success at getting thinner to criticize those who seemed out of control about their weight.

I couldn't tell if I'd hurt Giselle's feelings or not. The look she gave me was one of bewilderment more than anything else.

"But, Glenda, I thought you *loved* the idea of being a fashion model. Doing plus-teen modeling was your best bet for staying in it. If you don't gain the weight back . . ."

I leaned across the table. "Giselle," I said, "do you hear what you're saying? I know how hard you tried and how much help you were in getting me into modeling. So please don't think I don't appreciate it. But, well . . . . Which do you think I'd rather be? A fat-teen model or a normal-size teenage girl?"

Giselle just stared at me in a way I'd never seen her do before. Maybe she was thinking that, after all the support she'd given me, I was behaving like a traitor. But it was too late to back off. So I went one bold, now-or-never step further. "And, given a choice, which would *you* rather be?"

For the very first time since I'd known Giselle, I'd actually confronted her head-on with her weight problem. But why not? She had suggested that I should get fatter. So why couldn't I suggest that she should get thinner? Anyhow, wasn't it about time for us to stop talking about me and to start talking about her instead?

Gathering courage, I made my next words even more personal. "Admit it," I urged, as I watched Giselle nervously start to finger the glossy menu in front of her. "Can you really be happy going on the . . . the way you are now? Living out here in Havenhurst, trying to get settled in school and all?"

I didn't need to go into detail because I knew that Giselle was aware of the names people had been calling her behind her back, the goofy looks and sly grins they'd cast in her direction. And, despite her brave front, I knew that she'd been miserable from the first day she'd enrolled in Havenhurst Junior High.

I knew, too, that I couldn't help her simply by being at her side all the time. For one thing, I had my own life to live. There was my date with Roddy, in fact, for this very evening. There were my other friends, Mary Lou and especially Patty, with whom I was hoping to straighten things out at school on Monday. There was my hope of fulfilling all the dreams I'd had about what life would be like once I'd turned fourteen. All I could do was to try to help Giselle help herself, even if it meant that I might seem a little unsympathetic at times.

Just then the waitress came by and plunked down

two glasses of water. "Take your order?" she inquired.

Giselle looked up, her finger already pointing to one of the triple-peaked desserts in a boat-shaped dish, a sort of frozen-yogurt version of a banana split.

I placed my hand on top of Giselle's. "Why don't we wait another couple of minutes? Until my parents get here?"

The waitress flounced off, looking slightly annoyed.

"Answer me, please, Giselle. Did I just say something awful? Do you remember when I was first starting to get unhappy with the fat-teen scene and you told me that I shouldn't feel that way because I was being the best that I could be?"

Giselle gave me a sober look. "Yes, I remember. It was that day in the school cafeteria when you were getting antsy about whether they were going to ask you to be in the runway show at Ballard's."

"Right. And then they asked me. And it only made me feel worse. Because I knew I was going to be the token fatty in the show. And I went right on being unhappy about it until, little by little, I found out that I could be even . . . better than a fat-teen model. So how do we ever know what's the *best* that we can be? Unless we try."

Giselle picked up her glass and took a long sip of water. "Glenda, if you think I can start losing weight, you don't know what you're talking about. I never even *tried* to cut down before."

I leaned across the table enthusiastically and grabbed

Giselle by the shoulders. "That's all the more reason to be optimistic," I exclaimed. "You'll have no past failures to haunt you. Like I've had all my life."

I bounced back into my seat. "Oh, Giselle, promise me you'll try. It'll be good for both of us. If *I'm* the 'model' you're following, *I'll* be ashamed to get fat again. And if I help you at all, it'll be my way of repaying you for all you did for me."

By way of an answer, Giselle placed both hands squarely on the menu and slowly slid it away from her. "No frozen-yogurt banana boat, huh?" she said, her eyes beginning to dance the way they had when I first met her.

"Nope," I replied firmly. I turned the menu around and began running my finger down the special low-calorie list of Lite desserts. I was still searching for the frozen dessert with the lowest number of calories next to it when Giselle nudged me with her foot under the table.

"Are you ready for this, Glenda? Your parents are here." Giselle stood up to wave them in our direction.

The moment my mother spotted Giselle, she came rushing toward us with a harried air. My father strolled solemnly behind her. I could hardly keep myself from asking, "Who died?"

"Oh, Glenda darling!" my mother said mournfully, as she collapsed onto the seat alongside Giselle. She handed the Ballard's shopping bag she was carrying to my father, and he sat down beside me, carefully placing the bag on the floor between us.

"I hope that girl who tripped you was punished, severely punished," my mother declared. She leaned toward me. "Are you really all right, baby?"

"Stop fussing, Grace," my father said. "She looks fine to me. The girls have been waiting for us a long time. Why don't we order?"

"I *am* fine," I said, giving my father a loving poke with my shoulder. "In fact, things couldn't have worked out better."

My mother brightened a little. "Really? Ah, then Miss Oliver wasn't angry at you. There'll be lots more modeling opportunities at the store. Right?"

"Oh, lots more," I replied eagerly. "There's the summer fashions promotion. I think that starts in January, right after Christmas. Of course, I'll have to gain about twelve or fourteen pounds to be in it."

My mother looked startled. "Are you sure? That much?"

"Or," I went on, "Giselle might lose enough weight by then so *she* could be in Ballard's summer promotion."

My mother frowned, gave me a look of complete puzzlement, and buried her head in the menu.

"Hmmm," she murmured after a moment or two. "I'll bet I know what Giselle and I are going to have." She nudged Giselle lightly. "A frozen-yogurt banana boat, right?" She peered across the table at my father. "We can all afford to splurge a little, Harold, don't you think? You know, to celebrate Glenda's success."

"As I was saying," I continued, all too aware of my

mother's readiness to fall into the ways of temptation and drag Giselle along with her, "Giselle and I happened to be talking about modeling just before you arrived. We were being sort of philosophical, you know? And we agreed that modeling is a *lot* like life. Whoever you are, whatever you are, you have to keep on trying to be the best that you can be."

My mother gave me another perplexed look. At that moment, the waitress reappeared to take our order. My mother glanced expectantly at Giselle, waiting for her to go first. There was one of those awkward little pauses, when people can't quite make up their minds. At last, Giselle raised her head.

"I'll have a single scoop of Lemon Lite Delight," she announced in a clear voice, to the astonishment of both my parents. Then Giselle's eyes met mine, we exchanged a meaningful look . . . and she winked!